Emily Drake's heart was set on an impossible love.

"This is for you," he said, pressing a small object into her gloved hand. "A Christmas present. I've been working on it all week long."

"But," she started to protest, "I can't possibly take—"

"It's a gift," he said. "Of course you can take it."

"But. . .I. . .it's wrong to accept a gift."

"I want you to have it to remember me by."

Without saying another word, he jumped onto the buggy seat and shook the reins.

Emily's face, hot from his touch, stood as if suspended in space. Her heart soared as she watched through the darkened shadows at Ben Galloway's retreating back, riding off into the dark night. She unclasped the hard object, and held it out in front of her. It was a tiny horse carved from wood. It was beautiful, the hard wood soft and smooth. For her. A gift for her. And he had made it. She swallowed hard as she tucked it into the pocket of her winter coat.

He would be gone first thing in the morning and she wondered if she would ever see him again. He said he would return, but would he? Iowa was a long way from Oregon. There were extenuating circumstances. Ben's mother. A sister. Perhaps they wouldn't want to move out West. Perhaps they would talk Ben into staying there.

I'll wait, an inner voice said. *Yes, I will wait, though I know I shouldn't. Though I know it means trouble, I will wait.*

BIRDIE L. ETCHISON resides in Washington State. Her love for the beautiful countryside of the Pacific Northwest comes through in this historical novel set in Oregon's early 1900's. *The Heart Has Its Reasons* is Birdie's **Heartsong Presents** debut.

The Heart
Has Its Reasons

Birdie L. Etchison

Heartsong Presents

*In loving memory of my maternal grandmother,
the inspiration for this story.*

A note from the Author:
*I love to hear from my readers! You may write to me at the
following address:*

> **Birdie L. Etchison**
> **Author Relations**
> **P.O. Box 719**
> **Uhrichsville, OH 44683**

ISBN 1-55748-708-1

THE HEART HAS ITS REASONS

one

Emily Drake looked admiringly at the even rows of hand-dipped chocolates. With Christmas less than a fortnight away, she had put in a hectic week, working ten and twelve hours a day. Oregon's Finest Chocolates was a popular gift item. Not that she'd be receiving any candy from a suitor. At twenty-four, she had become resigned to the title of "Spinster." She supposed she'd still be dipping chocolates when she turned fifty.

Kate caught her attention from the next table. Smiling, she popped a small imperfect chocolate into her mouth and raised a finger to her red lips. "Sh-h-h," she whispered, her dark eyes flashing. "Don't tell now."

Laughing, Emily took a lopsided one from her row and bit into it. Maple creme. Her favorite. It was okay to eat an occasional chocolate, but she usually didn't. Working at the factory full-time took away any desire for the sweet confections.

Kate wiped her hands on her apron. "There goes a pound." Kate had a buxom figure which she constantly lamented about. "When I think of all the dresses in my closet I can't wear—I shudder. Look at you—slender as a stick—just as I used to be. I'm truly envious."

Emily's face reddened as it always did whenever she received a compliment. She never quite knew how to respond. Perhaps it was because she received so few. But getting acquainted with Kate these past two months had changed all that. Kate was fun. Daring. Talkative. And beautiful. Emily found herself eager to come to work, eager for each day to start, wishing she could be half as daring, half as beautiful.

"Are you sure you've never been married?" Kate had asked the day after they met. She stood at the production line next to Emily. Emily had been assigned to oversee her, making sure she dipped the chocolates just right. The fondant or caramel had to be completely covered, yet too much chocolate was a waste.

"I—" Emily hesitated, "have never had anyone come calling."

Kate's mouth opened in surprise. "I hardly believe that. You're attractive, even if you are shy."

Shy. The stock boy had said that about her when she turned down his offer to go for a buggy ride back when she first came to work here. That was in 1899. It was now December of 1907 and nobody had asked to come calling since. She rarely explained why she didn't date, the real reason being she couldn't see anyone who didn't belong to the Friends Church. Not that she couldn't, but that she wished not to. There was a difference. It was also her beliefs that kept her from going to dances though Kate had asked her twice now.

"Some day I hope to have a family," Emily said, pausing to look at her row of chocolates.

Kate rolled her eyes. "You have to get married first. And before you get married you are courted. There's another dance next Saturday at the Grange Hall. Why not go with me?"

Emily sighed as she dipped another mound of fondant. "I can't. I explained that already."

"This isn't just any old dance," Kate said. "They have food and toe tapping fiddle music. The people are friendly and this one man—his name is Ben Galloway—is so handsome and probably the best dancer I've ever seen."

"The Religious Society of Friends doesn't believe in any kind of dancing," Emily explained. "It's worldly and we do not partake of worldly ventures."

"Well, my goodness. Isn't that something! Quite frankly I can't imagine not being able to dance," Kate went on. "It's a good way to meet people."

"If you like this—this Ben so much, maybe you'll get married again," Emily said. She knew Kate was lonely. Being widowed at nineteen had been difficult. It was that loneliness that made her leave the farm in Cottage Grove and move to Portland. She didn't talk much about that period of her life, not even when Emily asked questions.

"Ben's not my type," Kate said. "We're too much alike."

Emily stared at her friend. How did one know if a man was her type or not? The concept sounded strange to her. But, then, she didn't think like Kate, nor did she dress like her. Kate wore her dark hair in tight curls that made her hair net spring to life. Emily's hair, neither brown nor black, was dull. Straight. Her mouth was too wide for her face, her nose small. Her eyes, the color of Persian violets, were her best asset. Not that she should be thinking about such things. Hadn't Grandmother said that beauty didn't count? "It's what's inside that matters, Emily."

Well, if it's what's inside, I guess that needs some changing, too, she thought now as she heard Kate exclaiming about the polka, her favorite dance.

"About the dance. . ." Kate was also persistent.

"Maybe I will go. Just once, mind you."

Once said, Emily couldn't believe the words had come from her mouth. Why had she agreed? How could she even consider it? The Friends would never understand. And how could she begin to explain what prompted her affirmative response? Besides, she didn't have the sort of

attire suitable to wear to a dance. Her wardrobe consisted
of two dresses: the simple gray cotton she wore to church
(it was plain; definitely not a dancing frock), and the brown
muslin, her every day dress. Faded and worn at the seams,
it looked like what it was: a work dress.

And if that wasn't enough reason, she didn't have the
slightest idea of how one danced.

"Oh, Emily, I'm so glad!" Kate bounded over, hugging
Emily hard. "You'll have ever such a nice time!" A smudge
of chocolate ran across one cheek still pink from rouge.

Rouge and lip coloring was something else Emily didn't
use. Another reason for not going to such social functions
as dances.

"I just finished my last chocolate," Emily said, removing her soiled apron.

"Me, too," Kate added.

"I must rush home. Grandmother likes to serve supper
at six." A sinking sensation hit the pit of her stomach. How
could she possibly get permission from her grandparents?
If she mentioned the word "dance" they would first pray,
then preach at her for hours.

"You always rush home," Kate said.

It was true. But there were chores to do. Wood to chop
and bring in for the night's fire. Water to fetch, the chickens and rabbits to feed.

Kate retrieved her wraps from the cloakroom hook. Her
blue-flowered dress flounced as she walked. She wore
several crinolines, even to work. Emily wondered how she
would look at a dance, a dress-up occasion.

"I can hardly wait for you to meet Ben. I have this inner
feeling that he's right for you."

That was something else. Inner feelings. Didn't Kate
realize that God put those feelings inside a person? It wasn't
luck or happenstance. When you believed, you stood ready

for His guidance and direction, what Friends called "inner light."

She moved past Kate. "I doubt that this Ben is a man of God. And that's important as the Bible teaches that a believer cannot be unequally yoked—"

"I didn't say you were going to marry him," Kate interjected.

Emily buttoned her threadbare coat, then reached for her hat. "Just the same, the possibility exists whenever you keep company with someone that this might be the one."

Only, if only she had heeded those words. If only she had listened to her convictions.

"We can't all go to the same church, believe the same things," Kate said then. "Maybe he believes in God. Why not give him the benefit of the doubt?"

"Sorry." Emily waved her hand in dismissal.

"Are you like those Quakers who pray in silence all day?" Kate, all five-feet, nine-inches stood in the doorway.

Emily tied the strings of her brown woolen bonnet, and reached for her gloves. "When George Fox, our founder, said: 'We tremble at the word of the Lord,' people started calling us Quakers, but we prefer the name *Friends*." Emily had heard the story countless times, and it always amused her.

"Come to meeting sometime, Kate. See what it's like for yourself. I play piano for the services."

Kate hugged Emily again, knocking the hat askew. They both laughed. It was one thing Emily liked about Kate. She was loving and kind. You could get into discussions and even though she didn't agree, she never became angry, never judged. She was the best friend Emily had ever had— the only friend. Emily knew she shouldn't bargain, but couldn't resist this one time. "Would you consider going to meeting with me? We could sit together and—"

"Write notes."

"Write notes?"

Kate laughed. "I'm teasing. I meant if the sermon got tiresome I might write or doodle."

Emily couldn't promise that it wouldn't be tiresome. When one wasn't familiar with the teachings of the Bible, or not used to praying, she supposed it could be tiresome.

"Of course I'll go, if only to hear you play."

It was settled then. Emily would go to the next dance on Saturday night, and Kate would attend meeting the following morning.

Kate headed west to catch the streetcar, while Emily caught the one heading east. While Kate's stopped at the corner next to her house, Emily had several blocks to walk since the tracks didn't go that far.

Emily could hardly believe Kate had agreed to accompany her to meeting. She had asked before, only to have Kate scoff, saying she didn't need any church telling her how to live, or what to wear. Kate wouldn't want to give up her brightly-colored dresses, the lip color and rouge, the rings or perfume. Yet if she understood the reasons, it might make a difference. Though Kate seemed happy, there was a restlessness about her, and Emily knew she needed God in her life. He could heal all hurts—big ones and little ones alike.

As Emily hurried the half-mile walk home, the evening air nipped at her cheeks. Winter would soon be here and with it came rain, winds out of the east and sometimes snow. She needed a new coat, but doubted that there would be enough money for one this year.

She thought again about dancing, what it must be like to dance with a man, to feel one's arms around you. Would she ever know love? Was there someone in her future? Or would she be like the Ditler Sisters who owned and operated the Dry Goods Store on Foster Road? It was where her grandmother bought material for their dresses. Always brown, gray and black. Never red, pink, or blue as Kate wore. She didn't want to remain a spinster, but if that was what God had in mind for her, so be it.

"Thee is late," Beulah said when Emily came in through the back door, bringing a gust of wind. "I've been holding supper."

Emily shrugged out of her coat. Both grandparents often slipped into the old way of talking, referring to her as "thee," and saying "thou" and "thine." Emily rarely used the terms now.

It was warm inside, and the lamp on the sideboard was lit, casting shadows across the kitchen. The smell of fried potatoes and freshly baked bread made her stomach tighten. She hadn't realized how hungry she was. "We stayed to finish an order that came in this morning. Mr. Roberts said it would be extremely busy for the next week."

"More money in thy check then." Beulah, a formidable woman with wide shoulders and gray hair pulled back into a severe bun, regarded her granddaughter. "Not that there will be enough for Christmas presents, however."

Yes, more money, which Emily never saw. She turned her earnings over to her grandparents as that was expected of her. Though most of her money was set aside "for a rainy day" as Grandmother put it, she often wondered what might happen to them if she were to marry and move out. Before she had been old enough to work, Grandfather had farmed the land, but as his rheumatism worsened, he planted less and only recently had sold several parcels of land, banking the proceeds. Now all that remained was the lot the house sat on, and a partial acre.

"Fetch the water, then we can eat," her grandmother said. Emily grabbed the bucket off the counter and hurried back outside. The water was crystal clear. Cold. She looked at the clumps of green grass poking through mounds of dried, brown maple leaves. The zinnias she'd planted earlier that spring were mere straggly stems with drooping heads. She'd plant more next year. And the year after that. Douglas fir dotted the landscape, giving protection against the bitter, east wind. It was this rugged Oregon country her great-grandparents had moved to from Missouri back in the mid-1800s. How she wished she could have known them. Were they as stern as Grandmother Drake? As quiet and deep-thinking as Grandfather? Would they have given up one of their daughters, sending her from California to live with grandparents? She blinked back sudden tears, as she carried the full bucket up the path toward the house. No sense in dwelling on things from the past.

The dinner didn't quite fill the empty space inside, but Grandfather cleared his throat, saying his usual litany, "'Tis better to leave the table a little hungry then too full."

The teakettle hummed on the stove. After washing the supper dishes, Emily worked on her quilt squares, sitting close to the kerosene lamp so she could see better. Grandfather might request she play some of his favorite hymns on the old pump organ, followed by a chapter or two from the Bible. Then it would be time to slip up the attic stairs to bed.

"Is something troubling thee, child?" Grandfather asked after Emily had played his favorite, "Count Your Blessings." Emily wasn't a child anymore. Would her grandparents ever see her or think of her as a woman? Yet she wouldn't correct her grandfather. He was old and set in his ways. He was also growing deaf. She wanted to run to him, question him about the dance, ask if he had ever once danced, but she didn't dare. She couldn't risk the anger, the accusations from Grandmother. She would never understand. Never.

"I am fine, Grandfather. Just a bit tired, I guess."

"It's nearly bedtime," Grandmother said from her corner where she rocked the evening hours away. "Thee can read one chapter of the Bible, then go up."

Emily's fingers touched the pages of the big book. She was reading Isaiah now and it tied in with the Christmas story.

"'For unto us a child is born, unto us a son is given, and the government will be upon his shoulder; and his name shall be called Wonderful, Counsellor, The Mighty God, The Everlasting Father, The Prince of Peace.'" (Isaiah 9:6)

"Bless Thy word, bless Thy holy name," Grandfather said as Emily closed the book.

She sat thinking about the Christmas story. She never tired of hearing it, and it warmed her heart as she thought about the promise of the coming Messiah, and how the Jews didn't believe that this precious infant was Jesus. Since they didn't believe that, they didn't believe in salvation, and Emily thought that was sad.

Emily bade her grandparents good night and headed for the stairway. Holding the lamp in one hand, lifting her skirts with the other, she climbed the steep attic steps. She *was* tired, but there would be time to pray, to write.

As the house settled to a quietness, Emily stared at the soft, steady glow of the lamp. It was wasteful to use the kerosene, but she must write in the diary. It was one of her few pleasures—something only she knew about. Something Grandmother could not be critical about.

Emily closed her eyes and thought of the dance. Even if it was a little more than a week away, she couldn't get it out of her mind.

She uncapped the bottle of India ink and dipped the pen.

Mama. Emily always addressed the small leather-bound book in that way. It was as if she was talking to her mother, and in turn her mother answering her. It wouldn't make sense to anyone else, and that's why it was a closely guarded secret.

> *I've been invited to a dance. I know I shouldn't have accepted, but something inside me said, yes, do it. Just this once. I want to see Kate dance, Mama. I want to hear the music. Is that so terribly wrong? Did you ever attend a dance? I also want to see this Ben Galloway Kate talks about. Now, that's wrong. I know it is, and yet something is propelling me on. . . Oh, what is to become of me?*

Emily wiped the nib clean and capped the ink bottle. Shivering, she blew out the light, burrowing under the heavy quilts on the four-poster bed. No heat came up the stairs, and as the wind howled outside, rattling the window, Emily was glad she'd read scripture downstairs in front of the fire.

After warming up just a bit, she flung the quilts back and kneeled on the small rag rug beside her bed—the rug she'd braided from old quilt scraps. She'd been twelve that year. She folded her hands and prayed. "Forgive me my transgressions, O, God. Let me be ever mindful that as Your child I must do what is right to bring glory to Your name. Amen."

It was a long time before Emily could shake the dance from her mind, and it wasn't until she'd made the decision not to go that she felt better. She would explain to Kate that it was wrong to put desires of the flesh before Godly things. It couldn't be helped, but she must decline. They could still be friends at work, couldn't they? Kate would have to understand.

two

It was a sleepless night. Though Emily prayed for forgiveness, declaring she wouldn't attend the dance, she knew it didn't matter. She had succumbed to a worldly desire, and though she might choose to stay away, the fact remained that she had wanted to go—*yearned* to go. And therein lay the problem.

When she left for work the next morning, she carefully rehearsed what she would say to Kate, how she would decline going to the dance.

But somehow she couldn't do it when she saw Kate's smiling face. Humming as she worked, Kate talked about different dances and how she had learned all of them since moving to Portland.

"My husband didn't like to dance. In fact the only thing he was interested in was farming. I discovered real quick that I wasn't a true farmer's wife."

Emily wasn't sure if she would make a good farmer's wife, if she'd make a good any kind of wife. She tried to tell Kate that she'd changed her mind about the dance, but she'd barely get one word out before Kate started talking again.

"Guess I'll wear my red dress to the dance since red is so Christmasy," Kate continued.

Christmas. There would be little celebration in the Drake household. Emily might receive a new pair of mittens or a scarf. She had no idea what her grandmother knit during the day while she was at work. Emily was working on an embroidered dishtowel set for Grandmother, and warm, woolen socks for Grandfather. He always complimented Emily's work, saying her stitches were tighter than Grandmother's.

"Don't thee tell her I said that," he would say once Grandmother was out of earshot.

Emily would nod and smile, knowing the last thing she would ever do was get Grandfather in trouble. And trouble there would be.

The past week Emily had worked on a muffler for Kate. A heavy black wool, it would lend warmth on cold, windy days. Kate preferred bright colors, but black yarn was all Emily had.

"About the dance," Emily began, her eyes not quite meeting Kate's.

"No," Kate said, interrupting her. "You're not going to back out, Emily. I knew this would happen and I won't let you do it."

"I don't have a red dress, or a green one either—"

"Of course you don't. And believe me, it doesn't matter."

"It's not right for me to go."

"I know you think it isn't, but you're going this once as a favor to me."

As a favor? How could Kate twist things around like this?

"Are God's promises worthless?"

Emily's cheeks flamed. "Certainly not!"

"Then how about yours? Shouldn't you be accountable for your promises?"

Emily stared at her friend. "Of course I should."

"Then I'm holding you to that promise."

"Now, Kate. You don't understand about the doctrine."

"And wasn't it the doctrine you escaped from in England back in the 1600s or whenever?"

"That was different," Emily protested.

"If so, how?"

Emily tried to remember how an older member explained it in meeting one First Day. "We want to better the world, and let ourselves shine as good examples."

"Attending a dance isn't going to send you to damnation, now is it?"

Emily hesitated. "No, that's not the point. How can I be a good example if I'm in a dance hall?"

"Grange hall," Kate corrected her.

"It's still a dance."

Kate sighed. "I sure don't want to be responsible for any wrongdoing, or for any guilt you'll feel."

"If I go, it will be to watch, not to dance."

"That's fine," Kate answered. "The music is good. You'll recognize some of the tunes. 'Turkey in the Straw,' 'Irish Jig,' and 'O, Susannah!' Refreshments are also served. Probably punch and cookies. I know it'd do you good to get out, but it's up to you."

The subject was closed for the time being.

Wednesday turned rainy. Grandfather said his rheumatism was acting up and he should stay home from prayer meeting.

"Thee stay home then, but Emily and I are going," Beulah announced.

Emily drove the wagon, not minding the fine mist coming down. Her hat with wide brim kept the rain off her face. She needed to talk to Grandmother about staying at Kate's Saturday, but the time wasn't right. Rarely was the time right when it came to discussions of any sort. Grandmother sat stiff and silent, so Emily remained quiet as well.

Maybe tomorrow would be better.

The hall buzzed with voices when they entered. The talk stopped abruptly when Beulah and Emily walked in. Myrtle Lee rushed over, linking her arm with Beulah's.

"We've just heard from Ohio. Pastor Luke Morrison is coming to Portland. He accepted our request. He was pastoring a meeting when his wife died, and he realized he couldn't stay there. Too many memories."

"Wife died?" Beulah repeated. "How old is this pastor?"

"Thirty-five, I believe someone said."

Emily felt several pairs of eyes on her. She knew what they were thinking. Could this be God's answer to her prayers? Might this be a prospect for a mate? She felt a twinge inside. How could she be thinking this way when they hadn't even met?

The bulk of prayers that night were for the man who would be among their midst soon. Times were changing. The old way said that one can discover true belief and righteous conduct from the inner light—that one did not need a minister to lead. Of late there was dissent.

"We are in the twentieth century," a younger man had proclaimed at the last yearly meeting. "With our growth, we need a preacher."

"And perhaps we should abandon our dark attire and drop the formal way of talking," someone else said.

"Never," Grandmother proclaimed under her breath. "I won't hear of it."

In the end, the agreement had been to search for the right man to teach the flock. As for the other two suggestions, they were tabled for the time being. It was up to each individual to do as he or she saw fit. And the meetings would continue opening and closing with silent prayers.

"Yes," Beulah said on the way home. "I think thy prayers

have been answered, Emily. Thee needs a husband. Pastor Luke needs a wife. He has had sufficient mourning time."

"Grandmother, I haven't even met this man."

"Thee will." Grandmother stared straight ahead. "It isn't good for man to live alone."

Nor woman, Emily said under her breath. Women get lonely, too. And loneliness leads you to do things such as attending dances. Now. She must ask when Grandmother seemed to be in a good mood. A bit of a smile played about her mouth.

"My friend Kate—from work—you remember my mentioning her?"

"Yes, thee has talked about her. Why?"

"She wants to go to church with me on First Day."

"Is she of our persuasion?"

"No, she isn't."

"Humph!"

Emily took a deep breath. "She. . .wants me to come for supper Seventh Day then we will walk to church the next morning—"

"Thee doesn't do much, I know."

Emily's heart soared. Was this her grandmother speaking?

"I expect it will be all right this once. If thee finishes all the Seventh Day work and the preparations for First Day."

Emily expected that. "I will," she murmured softly.

"But, I don't like the idea and might change my mind."

Emily swallowed. "She's a wonderful person, Grandmother."

"Still, I don't like you associating with people who don't believe as we do."

"Maybe she will come to believe, too."

It had been a thought, a wish Emily'd had, and who knew? Didn't God work in mysterious ways?

There was much discussion between her grandparents that evening, first about the new preacher coming, then about Emily staying with her friend for the night. Surprisingly, Grandfather was more opposed than she thought he would be.

"Thee better go to bed early Saturday night."

"I will, Grandfather," she promised.

Finally Emily crept up the stairs to bed to think and pray about the situation. She hadn't lied to her grandparents. She just hadn't told the whole truth. Would God forgive this transgression? She felt Him to be more forgiving than Grandmother and Grandfather. Not that they would find out. She certainly didn't see how.

For the remainder of the week, Emily's mind darted from the new preacher coming to thoughts of the dance on Saturday. She had never dipped so many chocolates. She even saw the rows of sweet confections in her sleep. Some day she might not be working in this candy factory. Some day soon she might marry, be the mother of a child, a child who would need her love, time, and attention.

Emily retired early on Friday night. No, she had told Grandfather. She felt fine, even if she did look a bit peaked.

When sleep didn't come, she crawled from under the heavy layer of quilts and tiptoed to the window to look out. No stars shining through the cloud layer. A lantern sent a tiny shaft of light bobbing in the still blackness as someone walked past the lane to the house. It was late. Most people were in for the night. Asleep. Just as she should be.

Her attention diverted, she thought of what it would have been like to share this room with a sister. Why hadn't her parents sent another child to stay? Why had they chosen her? Was it because she was imperfect in some way? What would happen if she went to California for a visit? Would they welcome her? What would her grandparents do? They had come to rely not only on her earnings, but on her help as well. Her thoughts turned to prayer.

"God, I need to learn the lesson of patience. Maybe I should read Job's story again—learn from his experiences. I remain Your child, Your servant. Amen."

The sheets were cold to her touch. Neither the long flannel nightgown or the cap that covered her head helped.

A sister would have helped warm her toes. They might have whispered in the darkness, shared secrets, giggled over the day's happenings. Emily shook the thought from her mind. It was quite obvious that a sister would never come from California. They were grown now.

There had been word at odd intervals. Letters penned in Mama's delicate scrawl. Little Olive Ann had died of a fever when she was but a year old. Paul had broken his arm. Maud, the spirited one, had married a few years ago. Mary was betrothed. Tom had moved away. Nobody seemed to know where.

The one time Emily had mentioned going home for a visit, Grandmother had scoffed.

"And pray tell, where would thee get the money for such a trip?" She stood, towering over Emily, hands on hips. "Goodness sake, child, thee should be grateful to have a roof over thy head. Doesn't thee know there are starving people in the world—those who would give anything to own two good dresses, to go to bed with food in their stomachs?"

Emily didn't broach the subject again.

And now that she couldn't sleep, she lit the lamp again.

She would write her thoughts down. One thing to be thankful for was the fact she never had to hide her diary. Neither grandparent would climb the steep steps.

She flipped back through her diary, reading passages from the first year after she'd come to Oregon.

The small leather bound book had been a presentation by her school teacher for winning the fifth grade spelling bee. It had been the most wonderful gift Emily had ever received, and she wrote in it that very night.

This book belongs to Emily Drake
The Year of our Lord 1893

That first entry read:

Mama,
How I miss you, Pa, and my brothers and sisters. I remember lying next to Maud with Mary on the other side. Across the room were the boys. Daniel with his straight blond hair, his mischievous grin. And Tom who chopped wood for each night's fire. Even now I can hear the ax sing, see the wood chips fly. Paul. He liked to be hugged more than anything. And Joel. How sick he'd get with the croup. Olive Ann. I remember the morning she was born. So tiny and red, and that plaintive cry.

Mama, I was the quiet, obedient one. Why did you send me away? Did you ever miss me? Did you cry when you saw my empty space between Maud and Mary? Do you think of me now, and wonder about how much I have grown?

Mama, I miss you so much. I remember your blue eyes, your plump, round shape. If only you could

*come to visit. Or send money for me to come on the
train.*

Emily didn't realize she was crying until something wet
hit her arm. No, there hadn't been money for train trips
then, or now.

She closed the diary as more memories filled her. Why
hadn't she written about the day she'd been bundled up
and driven to the train station with Mrs. Barnes, a lady
from church? Was it because the memories were too pain-
ful? Mrs. Barnes trilled on and on about how beautiful
Oregon was and how much Emily would enjoy being an
only child.

She remembered swallowing her tears and thinking she
didn't want to be an only child. She didn't care about
having her own room, receiving all the attention, the ad-
vantages. Why couldn't she have had a say in the matter?

She thought of Maud again. Kate made her think of
Maud. Maud had laughed a lot and liked to tease the
younger ones. Suddenly Emily knew Maud was too spirited to have lived here. She would have been whipped
every day and twice on First Day. Emily did as she was
told, and if tears or questions came to mind, they were
always repressed.

She blew out the light for the second time. Lying in the
darkness she listened as the rain whooshed from one side
of the house, then changing directions, whooshed back the
way it had come. Usually the rain lulled her to sleep, but
tonight was different. Tonight her thoughts kept sleep at
bay.

Tomorrow would come too soon as it was. She'd work
at the candy factory half a day, come home to do chores
around the house before leaving for Kate's. Grandmother

would put the beans to soak, and bake the bread, but Emily had wood to chop, and two buckets of water to fetch.

She planned to catch the last streetcar to Kate's. Together they'd have supper, and later attend the dance. She thought about Kate—Kate who wouldn't let her renege on a promise. Kate with the laughing eyes who was like a sister.

Sometimes God takes, but He always gives back. Yes, He always gives back. Smiling as she pulled the quilt up under her chin, Emily closed her eyes.

three

Now that she was really going to the dance, Emily wondered about her simple gray dress. Maybe it was just a barn dance, but people would stare when she came in with Kate dressed in red while she wore gray. The last thing Emily wanted was to be noticed. Still, it couldn't be helped.

At last the chickens and rabbits were fed, eggs gathered, wood chopped and brought in, and two buckets of water drawn and waiting on the kitchen counter.

She was putting on her wraps when Grandmother cleared her throat. Emily froze. Had she done something to displease her?

"We will see thee in the morning," was all she said. Emily nodded and hurried out the door before she might think of something else she needed.

Her cheeks were red from the cold when she arrived at Kate's. Kate greeted her, looking happier than usual. "Emily, guess what?" She took her coat and hung it up. "I found the absolutely most beautiful dress for you."

Borrow a dress? Emily had never done such a thing. What if she ripped it, or spilled punch down the front?

"It's velvet. A royal blue. Come see."

The dress lay on Kate's bed. Emily's breath caught in her throat, as she touched the soft material. With puffed sleeves, a pleated bodice, and tiny pearl buttons, it was the most gorgeous dress she had ever seen. "Oh, Kate, I *adore* it."

Kate's eyes twinkled. "I knew you would. And it's going to fit you so nicely." She held it up. "Just as I thought. The color goes perfect with your eyes."

So this was velvet. Emily was sure she had never seen or felt material as wonderful as this.

"It doesn't suit me because it has no flounce." She slipped it over Emily's head, standing back to examine it. "I'll cut about six inches off."

"Cut?" Emily looked shocked. "You can't cut this. You couldn't wear it again."

Kate grabbed the pincushion. "It's okay. Like I said, it's not my style. Just think of how elegant you are going to look." Elegant. Emily had never looked elegant in her life. Kate made Emily turn as she pinned it up.

"You know I might comb your hair in a different style."

Emily wore her hair two ways. Brushed out, then braided in one long braid before going to bed, or wound into a braided knot at the nape of her neck. No ribbons, feathers, flowers, or fancy clasps.

"Let's hem this after supper," Kate said. "Everything's ready, and I'm starved."

"It certainly smells wonderful," Emily said, not wanting to take her eyes off of the dress.

A table was set with a white linen tablecloth, matching napkins, and fine china.

"Wedding presents," Kate said, bringing a covered dish to the table.

"It's lovely." Emily pulled out a chair, hesitating as she looked across the table at Kate. Kate never prayed over her food at work, but Emily wouldn't feel right without asking God's blessing on the meal. Kate touched her arm, as if she knew, then bowed her head.

"Lord, bless this food, this house, and my dear, dear friend Emily. Protect us and guide us. Amen."

Emily opened her eyes, smiling. "I like short blessings.

Sometimes Grandfather prays so long the food gets cold."

Kate had baked light rolls. She passed a buttery cream sauce filled with chunks of ham, to spoon on top. Raw carrot sticks, dried grapes, and celery chunks rounded out the menu. Emily had never tasted anything so delicious and said so.

"You'll have to come again," Kate answered.

Tea was served in tiny cups with a floral design. Dessert was bread pudding with cream.

After lingering over the tea, Emily pushed her chair back. She felt full. Content. "I'll wash dishes."

"You'll do no such thing," Kate said. "We'll stack them in the dish pan for now. We have more important things to do. Remember the Sears & Roebuck Catalogue I was telling you about?"

Emily nodded. How could she forget when Kate constantly mentioned all the merchandise one could buy through the mail order?

The catalogue was enormous. Emily touched the cover. The only book allowed in the Drake household was the Bible. Once Emily brought home a book of poems from the library and Grandmother frowned. "This reading of untrue things can't be worthy or honorable of our God," she remarked. Emily had returned the book the next day, unread.

"This should be called the *Wish Book*," Kate said, "as I keep wishing for this and wishing for that."

Fascinated, Emily selected a bicycle she would like to own. Kate liked the bicycles, but wanted a sewing machine.

"I plan to order this machine," she said, pointing at a sleek model on page two hundred and fifty-two. "I've been saving my money and almost have enough now."

A sewing machine would be wonderful. Grandmother

had an old treadle style and it worked, but it looked nothing like this one with shiny black paint.

"I'll also pick out a new crinoline and some under things. You can't imagine how pretty they are."

Kate suddenly sprang to her feet. "It's getting late. We better get the dress cut, hemmed, and pressed."

The sound of scissors on the beautiful material made Emily cringe. Noting Emily's discomfort, Kate said, "It was sitting in my closet gathering dust, so don't give it another thought." She handed Emily a threaded needle.

Emily began sewing tiny stitches while Kate checked to see if the iron was hot enough to press.

"I can't keep this," Emily said then. "Grandmother would never allow me to wear it."

"More's the pity." Kate looked thoughtful for a moment. "But we'll worry about that later. Here, you press while I change."

At eight, the two were ready. The red taffeta had a wide, full skirt with white lace at the bodice. A cameo brooch was pinned at the throat while two rings, one a garnet, the other diamond, adorned Kate's fingers. Emily watched as she dabbed perfume behind her ears. It smelled of lilacs.

Emily smoothed out the skirt of her dress. She felt like a princess. Against Kate's advice, she had brushed and rebraided her hair, wearing it as she always did. Pink dots appeared on both cheeks. No rouge needed here, not that Emily would have agreed to use any.

"You *are* pretty with those high cheekbones." Kate made her turn around while she investigated all sides. "I truly mean it. What I wouldn't give for such a creamy complexion."

Kate had agreed to let a friend drive them to the dance, and they had grabbed bonnets and coats when the horses pulled up out front.

"Kurt, this is Emily," Kate said. "Kurt's recently moved here from Germany."

Emily saw how the young, blond man gazed at Kate with an intense look. Kate seemed oblivious, however, as he helped her into the buggy and gave Emily an assist as well. The three arrived just as the fiddlers began tuning their instruments. Several others had come, and a big fire roared in the fireplace. Chairs lined up along two walls and off to one side was the table with punch and plates of cookies. Red streamers decorated the room. She had never seen anything so pretty. Trembling, Emily followed Kate. Before Kate had a chance to introduce her to anyone else, the music started and Kurt took Kate's hand, leading her to the middle of the floor.

Emily sat in one of the chairs and watched while Kate danced every number. Breathless, at the end of one round, Kate came over, pulling on Kurt. "Emily, Kurt loves to dance. Do you want to try? He'd be a good teacher."

Emily shook her head. It didn't seem quite as wrong if she just watched and listened. "I'm doing fine, thank you. The music is wonderful."

The Virginia Reel started up and Kate ran off with Kurt in tow. "I can't imagine where Ben is," she called over her shoulder. "When he arrives, you'll know," she added.

And she did. The Reel had just finished and another round dance was beginning when the door opened. Emily sensed the sudden quietness though the music was still playing. Every head seemed to turn to view the tall, bushy-haired man who had strode in. Ben Galloway. It must be. He surveyed the dancing people as if looking for someone, then walked over to the refreshment table.

Emily watched, absorbed by the bulk of him. By the dress. His coat, a heavy wool, had a wide collar and huge buttons. The boots looked new, his jeans were bluer than most, and the flannel shirt a bright plaid. "He's Scottish, you know," Kate had said. "That's why we're friends, but that's all we are."

The music was over and seconds later Kate was at his side, giving him a hug. "Ben, I thought you weren't coming tonight," she trilled.

Emily winced. Kate was like that, hugging people all night. It was her way of expressing herself. Besides she knew everyone.

He smiled, taking her hand as the music started. It was fast. Maybe it was the dance Kate said she liked best. A polka. Kate and Ben started off across the floor, followed by a blaze of color as others joined in. Those who didn't dance laughed and stomped their feet, and clapped their hands. It was so merry. Before she realized it, Emily was clapping, too.

When the dance was over, Kate was grabbed by another man. Ben shook his head at a woman with bright red hair and walked toward Emily.

Emily looked down at her lap, knowing Ben was coming over, not knowing what she would say to him.

The boots stopped in front of her and she was forced to look up. "Miss Emily Drake?"

"Yes." Her voice sounded unusually clear. Strong.

"Ben Galloway here. Kate would have introduced us, but as you can see she is the one every man wants to dance with. And no wonder."

Emily laughed, happy to have the attention drawn away from herself. "Yes, she's so light on her feet. And dancing makes her happy."

"And you, Emily? What makes *you* happy?" His eyes met and held hers for a long moment. She felt the blood rush to her cheeks as she finally looked away.

He stood, as if waiting for her answer. What could she

say? She didn't know what made her happy. In all honesty she had never thought about it much. Maybe she'd never been happy. If laughing and dancing was part of it, she doubted she would ever know. Going to meeting satisfied her. She knew she was a child of God, that He loved her and watched over her. That gave a sense of satisfaction. But happy? Perhaps writing in her diary qualified. Or laughing with Kate at work over something trivial.

"Not much, I daresay if it takes you this long to come up with an answer." He pulled a chair over and sat beside her. His presence overwhelmed her. She'd never looked into such vivid brown eyes, gazed upon such thick, bushy eyebrows. And the hair. It looked as if he'd combed it, but somehow it didn't matter. It was going to stand up like that because it was thick, and had a mind of its own.

"I enjoy reading," she finally said. "And writing. In my diary."

A smile flashed across his broad face. "Ah, a writer. A reader. Both worthy endeavors. And I understand from Kate you're the best chocolate dipper in town."

She blushed more than before. "I don't quite agree."

"You are an educated young lady, I can see, and a pretty one, too. Not too many can lay claim to both."

Emily had the sudden impulse to run. Her throat felt dry and her hands seemed to be twisting in her lap.

"I want to dance with you, Emily."

"I—I don't dance."

"Of course you do. Everyone dances."

"No, it's against my beliefs."

"Which are?"

"I belong to the Society of Friends and we feel that dancing is wrong—"

"So, what brought you here?"

"Kate insisted. And since I promised, I had to come.

Just this once." She didn't go on to tell him how persistent Kate had been, or how much she wanted her to have fun.

"Anyone in such a beautiful dress has to dance at least once."

Emily could see he wasn't going to go away until she agreed.

"I'll request a waltz, because it's one of the easiest to learn." He pushed a stubborn lock of hair off his forehead. "Then I'll show you how to waltz. We won't say you danced. You can say you waltzed."

Emily began stammering, but Ben had walked across the floor and spoke to the musicians.

The slower music started and Emily felt herself being drawn from the chair and into the stranger's arms.

"It's simple. A one-two-three, then one-two-three as we turn. We do the one-two-three repeatedly and waltz around the room. Just like this."

She felt tiny in his arms, her forehead reaching the middle of this thick chest. While his right arm encircled her waist, his left arm guided her into the moves. The one-two-three was easy. It was the moving about that took careful concentration.

"There. You are doing splendidly." He tilted her back so he could see her face. "Smile, Emily. This is supposed to be enjoyable."

But how could it be enjoyable when she felt her heart tripping away against the bodice of the blue velvet. She could barely breathe, and she felt as if she might float away.

Then he was humming the tune, his breath in her hair as she trembled against him.

"I grew up in Iowa, and the first time I went to a barn dance, my older brother taught me to waltz. That's why this will always be my favorite dance."

"Iowa?" Emily repeated.

"Yes. I'll be returning one day soon, on the train this time."

The train. Emily thought of her plans to take the train to California to see her family. The corners of her mouth turned up ever so slightly at the thought of seeing her parents again.

"See? You can smile, Emily Drake." He held her even closer. "And you dance wonderfully considering you never tried it before. I think you were teasing me."

"Oh, no." Emily stopped and stepped back. "I wouldn't tease about such a thing. And I don't lie."

The music stopped and Emily's heart beat even faster. "I have never danced. I. . .shouldn't be here now. . ." Emily realized they were the only ones on the floor, and in utter frustration, she tore out of Ben's arms and whirled off the floor and out the door. Tears pressed against her eyelids as she realized what she had done. Not only had she come to a dance, but she had actually danced with a man. Or waltzed, as he called it. And she had *liked* it. How could she like something that was wrong?

Ben was at her side, apologizing. "I am sorry, Emily. I would never want to cause you pain. But I won't say I am sorry for the dance. I enjoyed it and will think of you every time I hear 'The Blue Danube Waltz'."

Emily looked away. "I must go home."

"There's more than an hour left to dance."

"I—must go," she repeated.

"Then let me see you home."

She went to the room to fetch her coat and hat. "Thank you, Mr. Galloway, but I'd rather walk."

"I have a buggy outside."

"No. It's not far and it will help clear my head." A verse came to mind, one from Psalms. *I have gone astray like a lost sheep. Seek thy servant; for I do not forget thy com-*

mandments. (Psalm 119:176)

"Kate won't be leaving until the last dance is over."

"I know. That's fine. I know my way."

"May I see you again—say in some other way—not on the dance floor?"

Emily wanted to say yes; she longed to say yes, but it would be wrong. Surely God had not put this man in her path. He was not to be her prayed for husband because she had met him at a dance. God was sending someone else her way, someone who believed as she did and would be a good mate.

"I have a friend," she said then. It was true. Pastor Luke Morrison would be a friend. He would also be her minister. And it was to him she could go to pour out her heart, her troubles. Ask for forgiveness for her wrongdoing.

Ben cleared his throat. "Kate told me you didn't have any men friends. I naturally assumed this to be correct."

"She doesn't know about this one."

"Oh. Someone new then."

Ben stood back and watched the tiny woman at his side. He had danced with scores of women since he could remember, since the first time older brother Jesse introduced him to dancing, but he had never felt this way about any of them. He had always been sought after as a dancing partner, but none of the faces came to mind now. Kate, though beautiful and lively, was a good friend. He could talk to her about anything, but there it ended. There was no special feeling between them. Not like he felt about this woman. He had this sudden urge to protect her, to fight her battles, whatever they might be. From the frown on her face he knew she must have lots of them to fight. He also knew he wasn't going to find them out if he didn't change his tactics.

Emily lifted her chin and gazed up at him. She was

proud. A fighter. He had known that at first glance.

"Mr. Galloway, I really must go now."

He tipped his hat and watched while she trudged across the worn path, past the horses and wagons. His heart ached. His whole being ached with the sudden desire to run after her, to take her into his arms and to kiss those soft lips.

"Good-bye, Emily," he called out after her, watching as she sidestepped mud puddles, lifting her dress carefully. Then he went back inside.

The night was clear and as Emily walked a prayer began forming. "Please still my heart, O Lord. It was wrong what I did tonight. I realize why now. This man, this Ben Galloway is a wonderful dancer, but I know nothing about his other attributes. He cannot know You, Father, or he wouldn't have been at that dance. He cannot believe that I know You for what sort of witness was I tonight? Oh, please, please forgive me."

The tears began falling as she walked to Kate's. The velvety dark sky that usually intrigued her with its canopy of stars only troubled her more. Now she wished it were raining. Rain would help her forget her sorrows. Rain would also help cleanse her spirit. Tomorrow she would pray at Meeting, but for tonight she would read and repent. Read. Did Kate even have a Bible in the house? If so, she had not seen one. But how could one not have God's Word? Here she boasted of the Sears & Roebuck Catalogue, but probably didn't own a Bible.

Emily slipped into the back door and closed it gently. Falling to her knees, she began praying in earnest, then recited the Twenty-third Psalm: "'The Lord is my shepherd. . . he leadeth me in the paths of righteousness for his name's sake. . . .'"

David's plea in Psalm 51 came to mind next: *Create in me a clean heart, O God, and renew a right spirit within me. Cast me not away from thy presence, and take not thy holy Spirit from me. Restore unto me thy joy of thy salvation. . . .*

But nothing soothed her, or calmed her pounding heart.

She began washing the dishes, swept the floor. Anything to keep busy. Tomorrow she would feel better. Tomorrow would bring the forgiveness she needed so desperately. Her silent prayers would be lifted to God. In the presence of others she would surely feel His comfort. But tonight all she saw was Ben's face over and over again, feeling the touch of his hand as he guided her into the steps, seeing the smile that took over his whole face. And the hair. That impossible, thick thatch of hair that made a giggle slip out of her mouth as she remembered it.

Ben was not only in her mind, but was part of her heart as well. Without realizing it, he had captured her heart in a way she had never thought possible. She, a child of God, had fallen for the beguiling charm of a heathen, a nonbeliever. This wasn't as bad as blasphemy, but close. She had become part of the world, enjoying worldly things and it was the one thing the Friends talked about, how they were inspired by God to do good, to better the world, to change things, and Emily certainly hadn't held up her end. She had thrown caution to the wind and now would pay the consequences of having that memory embedded in her forever. The memory of waltzing with the best dancer in Multnomah County. The man with the twinkling eyes and the bushiest eyebrows she had ever seen. It would be a long while before she would forget Mr. Ben Galloway.

four

Emily was wakened by the sound of horses and a carriage pulling to a stop in front of Kate's.

She'd been lying on the sofa with a quilt around her lap, the lamp burning dimly. She hadn't planned on falling asleep, but it had been a full day and evening.

Kate's voice was calling good-bye, then footsteps ran up the porch steps. A rush of wind came in with her.

"Emily?"

"In here." She pulled to a sitting position. The velvet dress laid across a chair where she could admire it.

"Why did you run out like that?" Kate leaned over and turned the lamp up. "Are you sick?"

"Oh, no, nothing like that."

"You could have at least told me you were leaving."

Emily felt the sting of tears against her eyelids. "I'm sorry, Kate. That was very rude of me."

Kate sat and unbuckled her shoes. "I didn't mean to make you feel bad. It's just that I was worried. Of course Ben explained that you wanted to leave and insisted on walking home alone."

"It was a nice night."

Kate sat with shoes off, and began removing her jewelry. First the garnet brooch, then a thin silver bracelet. "Ben wants to see you again."

"I. . .I. . ." But Emily couldn't get the words out.

"Don't you think he's nice?"

"Yes, but—"

"And totally polite."

"Oh, yes, the perfect gentleman."

"And how about the dance? You waltzed wonderfully out there, Emily. You two never missed a beat."

Emily's cheeks flushed, and she could feel the pounding of her heart against her rib cage. "I looked good because Ben is a marvelous dancer and easy to follow." And once again, in her thoughts, she was in his arms and counting the one, two, threes under her breath. It seemed she had been crushed against his chest, but she had liked the feeling. It was safe. Comforting. And it was that thought that worried her, nagging at her that it wasn't—couldn't possibly be right.

"The dress made me look good, too," she finally said.

Kate leaned forward. "Emily, I'm giving you a compliment."

Her cheeks flushed brighter. "I know you are, but it's. . ."

"All you need do is say 'thank you.' Isn't that easy?"

Emily nodded. Yes, it was easy. If she could just think of the right thing to say at the precise moment, but it never came to her. Perhaps it was because Grandmother had done most of her thinking, and talked for her, too.

Four years ago, Grandmother Beulah thought she had found the perfect match for Emily. Jacob Halvorsen and his mother were new to the area. He was unmarried. Thirty-five years of age. Not bad looking, but painfully shy. Emily remembered how Jacob stood back while his mother told him what to say. Emily, equally shy, watched from the sidelines while Grandmother spoke for her. Jacob said one sentence to her, then looked as his mother coached him on what to say next. Then Beulah gave Emily the answer.

Emily pulled away first, knowing if she'd married someone like Jacob, it would be his mother running his life and Grandmother would continue to run hers. She didn't want that.

"Ben left right after you did," Kate said, "though I can't possibly imagine why."

"He did?" Emily couldn't hear his name without trembling. "I can't imagine why either since there was another hour of dancing, and he arrived late."

"I think he was smitten with you—"

"Kate, no!"

Kate merely smiled. "And speaking of smitten, guess who wants to come calling?"

"Kurt?"

Kate began rubbing the arch of her foot. "Yes, but I'm not ready to think about marrying again."

"He seems like a nice fellow, but you are still hurting inside."

"And missing Charles so terribly much."

"It takes time," Emily said, reaching over to touch her friend. She didn't know about losing a husband, but she'd lost her whole family and sometimes she wondered if time would ever ease the gnawing hurt.

"I like Kurt, though, so I told him he could stop by and take us to church in the morning."

Kate's words slammed into her. "Go to meeting with us?"

"Well, yes. That *is* all right, isn't it?"

"Oh, yes, of course." Emily sat lacing her fingers, then unlaced them again. How could she tell Kate she hoped it would be Ben coming by in the morning. Not that he would have wanted to attend meeting. He was far too worldly for meeting.

"I'm going to coax a fire out of the embers because I

need a cup of strong, hot tea." Kate flounced into the kitchen and seconds later she poked a stick of wood into the stove.

"Make a cup for me, too, please."

"Of course. I was going to do that automatically."

Emily crossed the room and touched the velvet dress. It was so beautiful and she'd felt like a princess. It was a memory she'd have forever. Just as she would remember the one time she'd danced, or "waltzed" as Ben called it. She would rock in her chair by the fire when she was old and wrinkled and tell anyone who would listen about the night she'd gone to a barn dance.

Emily tried to still the sudden beating of her heart, as she remembered sweeping across the dance floor, Ben leading the way. It was like magic, not that she'd ever had anything magical happen to her, nor did she even believe in magic. It didn't matter that her hair was plain, her shoes not fancy, nor that she was void of jewelry or a splash of perfume. Her dress had been elegant and for one small moment she, Emily Drake, felt beautiful.

Then came the shock. Like Eve eating the apple. How wonderful it must have tasted. But she had to pay for her sin. Banished from the Garden of Eden. Emily wouldn't be banished. God forgave people of their sins. It would be difficult, though, just trying to get the moment out of her mind, the memory of the waltz and how it had felt to be in the arms of a man.

Kate had changed into a nightdress and robe, and her hair was free of the sparkling combs. "I feel better now," she said. "Those corsets kill me."

Emily didn't own a corset, but perhaps one day she might need one. The peppermint tea tasted good and Emily felt her muscles relax. She certainly hadn't retired early as Grandfather had requested. She'd never stayed up past midnight before, and it felt strange, yet marvelous.

Kate set her cup down. "You need to get away from your grandparents, Emily. Start living your own life. Sure, I know that young unattached women must be chaperoned, but you're not exactly young anymore. And time is a definite consideration here."

Emily sat up straight. "I owe a lot to my grandparents. I could never just walk out the door. You don't understand how it is."

"Then explain it to me."

Soon Emily was pouring out her heart about when she'd first come to live with them, how much she missed her parents, her brothers and sisters, and how she had hoped that some day she would be able to see them again. If she could only get to California.

"Oh, Emily, how tragic." Kate put her arms around her, drawing her close. "I had no idea. I don't know how you've managed to survive."

"Do you think it's wrong for me to want to go to California?" Tears crowded the blue eyes.

Kate pressed a clean, white handkerchief into her hand. It smelled of lilacs. "No, I certainly don't. I'm just wondering how I can get you on the train and down there."

Emily started telling about her baby sister dying and the oldest one marrying, and that Mary was betrothed now.

"We receive letters several times a year."

"Well, I should certainly hope so. I can't believe they haven't come to see you. And wouldn't your father have wanted to visit his own parents?"

"Traveling is expensive."

Kate took the cups and set them in the sink. "And to think I complained about losing my husband. I'm sorry. Everyone has a burden to bear it seems, some burdens are heavier. It makes my wish for a sewing machine or running water small and insignificant by comparison."

If only Emily dared wish for things. Her wishes were more in the form of prayers, and over the years the only wish was to see her family once more.

Kate leaned over and kissed the top of Emily's head. "I hope you'll be comfortable in the spare room. Wake me when it's morning. I tend to sleep in."

Emily didn't sleep for a long time. After saying more prayers, thoughts of Ben crowded her mind. She didn't want to think about him, she had prayed she wouldn't, but the idea of seeing him again some time made the feelings resurface. What would tomorrow bring?

ও

Dazzling rays of sun hopped and skipped across Emily's face, wakening her. It was early, and the day showed promise of continued sunshine and warmth.

She shivered. If there was wood, she could build a fire. She stopped, remembering they hadn't prepared food last night, and she shouldn't cook or work on the Lord's Day, but water could be heated on top of the heating stove.

The fire started easily, and in a matter of minutes, the rousing fire warmed the small house. Coffee perked in the pot, and it was the smell that must have roused Kate.

Putting an arm into her robe, Kate stumbled into the kitchen. "I haven't had anyone make me a cup of coffee since I left home, and Mama was the first up and got the fire going."

There was a small amount of pudding left and a handful of dried grapes. It would do, especially with coffee and cream, Emily decided. She had dressed and brushed and braided her hair. No dillydallying as Kate did. She was ready and waiting when Kurt arrived.

Emily answered his knock while Kate hollered from the bedroom. "I'm not finished with dressing. Entertain him, Emily."

Emily swallowed. She couldn't entertain Kurt. What could she possibly say to him? She never knew what to say. She'd learned a long time ago it was better to let others do the talking. Like last night. The only time she talked to Ben was when he asked a question. She felt awkward, but it was even more awkward to let his questions go unanswered, especially when he stood over her, watching and waiting.

"I hear you play the piano," Kurt said, breaking the silence.

"Yes, I do. I've never had lessons, though."

"You can play by ear then."

She nodded. "Yes, I guess that's what they call it."

"That's remarkable. I have no ear for music. Can't even sing. I look forward to hearing you."

Emily nodded. She was going to tell him that it had only been in the last few years that here in the West the Friends' Society allowed music in the meeting, and people began having organs or pianos in their homes, but Kate flounced out of the bedroom and across the room. "You are a dear, Kurt, to be so patient. Thanks for keeping him company, Emily."

"It's so nice of you to come pick us up," Kate went on. "It will be the first time I've attended a Friend's church. How about you?"

"Same here." Kurt folded the rim of his fedora, then straightened it out again. "I started meeting with a Lutheran congregation after arriving in Portland."

His eyes never left Kate as he watched her every move. "You look. . .beautiful," he finally said.

Resplendent in a full-skirted pink-flowered dimity, Kate's lips were red, her cheeks rosy with rouge. Her hair, brushed high on top and decorated with pink ribbons, was soon covered with a wide-brimmed hat. Emily agreed with Kurt's comment.

At last they were on their way. Emily in her simple gray dress and hat, Kurt in a dark suit and stylish fedora, ordered from the Sears' Catalogue, and Kate looking positively regal. It was the nicest dress she owned, not counting the red taffeta, she claimed. She'd stand out, Emily knew, but it would be all right. She was a visitor. After the stares, people would settle down to the reason they came to meeting in the first place: to pray and worship God.

The meetinghouse was full when they arrived. Horses were hitched to the fence around the meetinghouse and Kurt had to leave his at the end of the line. The two women waited patiently for him to help them down from the carriage, then stood beside the front door.

A man smiled when he saw Emily, nodded to Kate, and offered his hand to Kurt.

"Thee can find room on this side, down in the front pew where Emily sits," he said pointing to the left. Kate raised her eyebrows, then followed Emily to the front row.

Emily could feel eyes on them, though most were in silent prayer. She slipped into the pew and lowered her head.

The meetings always began with silent prayer. Then Emily would slip out of the pew, go to the piano and open with a rousing hymn. She was shy until her fingers hit the keyboard. Then she was at home as she played a medley of songs. She ended with her favorite, and one she thought Kate would like: "What a Friend We Have in Jesus."

Guests were introduced and Emily heard a couple words

of exclamation when Kate stood. Her bright dress definitely made her stand out. Kurt's suit was appropriate, but his fedora was much more stylish than the hats most of the members wore.

The prayers went on longer than usual, or so it seemed to Emily. She glanced sideways at her friend, wondering if she would start writing notes. But Kate's eyes were closed and Emily saw a tear roll down one cheek. As Kate's mouth moved, she removed her handkerchief and dabbed at her face. Emily closed her eyes and took hold of Kate's hand. Kate squeezed back.

No longer did Emily feel distracted. She had prayed for forgiveness, but now prayed for her friend's problem. Her heart. Her soul. Suddenly Emily's prayers seemed inconsequential.

Later, as they headed up the aisle, Kate whispered, "Now I understand, Emily, why you believe. I truly felt God's presence today. Thank you for inviting me and for praying for me."

"You knew I was praying for you?" Emily asked.

The feather on Kate's navy blue hat pointed skyward. "Of course I knew."

Emily smiled. "I hope you come again, Kate."

"And I loved your playing. Your fingers go up and down that keyboard so fast, it took my breath away. I never saw anyone play with such energy, such verve."

Kurt had gone out to get the carriage. Kate waved her handkerchief, then hurried over, holding her hand so he could help her up. Emily called out good-bye, then joined her grandparents at their wagon.

"Isn't thy friend unmarried?" Grandmother asked.

"She's a widow," Emily said.

"Then who is this man with her?"

"He's just a good friend."

"But she's too young to be unchaperoned."

Emily didn't answer. It wouldn't matter what she said, Grandmother would find something to disagree with.

"Did thee have a good visit?" Grandfather was at her side, touching her arm.

"Yes, Grandfather, I had a wonderful time."

"Thee was missed," Grandfather added. "I'm glad thee enjoyed thyself."

Emily felt good and warm on the way home. The sun was shining out of a clear blue winter sky. Christmas was in three days. Grandmother would bake special sugar cookies to have with their morning tea. There would be additional prayers, and more reading from the Bible, but it would be the Christmas story and she never tired of it.

As for songs, she would play Christmas carols. "Silent Night, Holy Night," "Hark the Herald Angels Sing," and "O, Little Town of Bethlehem." The afternoon would be spent quietly, then the Drakes would attend Fourth Day night prayer meeting, Best of all, there would be no work that day or the next.

"We're almost out of wood," Grandmother said, as she lighted from the buggy. "I know it is Sunday, but thee can bring in an armful before dinner."

Emily looked at the farm house. A large two-story, it looked plain with its weathered gray boards, but it was home to Emily. She had enjoyed staying with Kate, but for some strange reason, something she couldn't quite explain, it was good to be home. She was used to the simple way of doing things. Austerity. Prayer time. Quiet First Day afternoons. This was part of Emily's life. She felt shame now to think she had dreamed about a man such as Ben. Ben with his expensive clothes, his splendid horse and buggy, while her grandparents owned an old horse and a plain wagon with a worn canopy.

Yes, this was her life, the one God intended for her to live. Kate had her life and though they could still be friends, Emily knew she'd never fit into Kate's world. There was no sense in even thinking about it anymore—in dreaming about Ben Galloway—or remembering the way his eyes seemed to tease her into thinking she was special. He was handsome, but he wasn't right for Emily. It was that simple. And with that thought, she went to gather wood for the stove, a job she could do and do well. One couldn't waste time thinking about things that weren't meant to be. Her home, her position in life was to be an upstanding member of her church, and community. And maybe, just maybe the new preacher would be the person for her. He was coming soon now. Would she feel about him as she felt about Ben? Or would she feel more stable, more controlled? She was sure the latter were true. If God had His hand in it, she would know, yes, Emily would know. She was certain it was Providence that brought Pastor Morrison to Oregon. Emily did not believe in luck. No. It was an answer to prayer—all part of God's timing, the way God took care of His people.

Emily stood, looking into the sky, breathing in the cold, clear air. Was her life beginning to change? Was it possible that one day she might take the train to California to see her family again? The thought made her tremble. She looked forward to seeing Kate at work tomorrow, just as she looked forward to meeting the new pastor when he arrived next week. A tiny part of her thought of Ben again, but she shut the idea out. He couldn't be part of her life. It wasn't right.

Filling her arms with split wood, she headed for the house.

five

Monday Emily had already finished a row of chocolates when Kate arrived.

"Kurt gave me a ride," she said.

"It sounds as if he's pursuing you."

She grinned. "That he is."

"Are you beginning to like him now?"

"Somewhat. But not in the way he wants."

The day went swiftly while they spoke of meeting and the way Kate had felt God's presence. "Maybe I do need God in my life, Emily, but I'm not ready to give up my beautiful dresses, jewelry, or rouge."

Emily smiled. She had heard people make that comment before. It was something Kate needed to struggle with on her own. It wouldn't matter what Emily thought or said about the matter. It was an individual choice. That's what the Society of Friends believed.

At closing, Emily heard what she thought was a familiar voice and looked up as Ben Galloway strode into the room. Her cheeks flushed, and she suddenly didn't know what to do with her hands.

"Hello, Kate. Emily."

His eyes fastened on hers and her heart did a flip.

"Hello," she finally stammered.

"What brings you here?" Kate asked, removing her hair net. "As if I didn't know."

"I came to take Emily home, you, too, if you want."

"Oh, I couldn't," Emily interjected. "It isn't proper that

I should go with you."

"Not even to see my new team of horses, and the carriage I bartered for?"

"Well, *I* want to see the new horses," Kate said. "And I also want to hear all about this bartering."

Ben glanced at Emily with a hopeful look.

Kate took his arm. "I've got the perfect solution to that problem. You can take Emily home and then me. That way she has a chaperone."

Emily's heart beat hard against her dress. "Yes. That would be appropriate."

"I'll sit in the back and not even listen," Kate said, fluffing her hair out.

"I think I should sit in the back," Emily said.

Ben looked down at her. She was even more beautiful than he remembered. Without a trace of rouge, her skin was smooth and clear, her cheeks a natural pink. The hair, parted in the middle, was braided, the way it had been Saturday night. He had memorized the way she looked, and the eyes—the eyes that had captured his interest— were now staring at him with that same look. All he wanted to do was touch her hand. Take her home. Walk her to her door. Speak with her. But it wasn't going to be easy. He could certainly see that now.

What need he do to win her approval? For him to call on her? Speaking to her grandfather was the first step. Kate was serious when she said Emily needed a chaperone. Most parents believed that, but Emily wasn't a young girl. She was a woman, in need of love, a husband, marriage and family. He had sensed that from the first moment they met. Yet her mouth was telling him no, as her eyes said yes, yes, yes.

He helped her with her coat.

Emily took a deep breath. She had to. She couldn't let Ben know what she was thinking. She couldn't believe she was thinking any of these thoughts, noticing again how vivid his eyes were, the thick hair that appeared unmanageable, the air of confidence that penetrated his being. How could this be happening to her? Why hadn't she heeded her own advice? Hadn't she worked it all out in her mind, convincing herself that she didn't need Ben in her life, let alone her thoughts?

Unequally yoked, unequally yoked, kept whirling through her brain as he took her arm and helped her into the carriage.

The horses were sleek. Two fine black horses with white markings. They appeared identical. They raised their heads as Ben approached and gave each a lump of sugar.

"They expect it," he said. "And I want to keep them happy."

Kate laughed. "I think you'd make anyone happy that was part of your life," she said.

The words weren't lost on Emily. She might be considered naive, but she caught the meaning.

The carriage was more of a surrey with a square roof covering everyone, even the driver. A bit of fringe dressed it up and the seats were of black, glossy leather.

"I've been thinking, though, about trading these in for an automobile. It's the best way for getting around these days."

"An automobile?" Kate trilled. "Really? That's a wonderful idea, Ben. I rode in one once and nearly lost my hat, but it was fun. A real adventure."

"It would be an adventure, all right," Ben said, his eyes twinkling as he glanced over at Emily. She remained motionless in the seat beside him and he longed to reach out and touch the side of her face, make her look at him instead of straight ahead on the road.

"I get the second ride, after Emily, of course."

Emily felt her face redden, as she put a gloved hand to her mouth. "Don't be silly, Kate. Ben's your friend. You knew him first. You definitely get the first ride." And even as she said it, she wondered how she would explain the fine horses and fancy carriage to the grandparents, let alone a car with an engine, in the event that she should ever actually ride with Ben. This was happening way too fast. And what was she going to say to Grandmother who would most certainly be watching from behind the curtained window in the kitchen?

"I've found a partner," Ben was saying, breaking into her thoughts. "We've just finished the Talbot mansion. I build cabinets, you know. This is the Talbot's old carriage and team. Seems Mr. Talbot bought an automobile and it arrived yesterday. This was in payment for all my hard work in the study. They have countless books, so I built fine oak shelves on three walls."

Books. What Emily wouldn't give to own one book, let alone numerous ones. It would be so wonderful, so leisurely to be able to read. And it surely couldn't be a sin as Grandmother suggested. "Idle hands are the devil's workshop," was one of Grandmother's favorite sayings. "I don't believe there's time for reading unless it's God's Word."

They came to the road leading into the lane where the Drakes' farmhouse stood. Emily touched Ben's hand. "I'd like to get out here, please."

"What? So you can walk in that mud?" His twinkling eyes met hers. "What sort of man would I be if I didn't walk you to your door?"

Fear rose in Emily's breast. She couldn't chance her grandparents meeting Ben. At least not yet. She had to think of explanations, reasons for his being there.

"Stop!" she commanded in as loud a voice as she could muster. She hopped out of the carriage, before Ben could put the reins down and walk around to assist her. She knew it wasn't lady-like, but if she hurried in, she would fare better.

"Thank you for the ride." She readjusted the skirt of the brown dress, avoiding his eyes, knowing the gaze was still there, the gaze that had a way of captivating her, making her thoughts all tangled up inside.

"I want to see you again tomorrow," Ben called out as Emily hurried up the road. "Lord willing," he mumbled under his breath.

Emily began bracing herself for the barrage of questions she knew would be forthcoming. Grandmother could see the side road from the kitchen window, and this time of day always found her busy with preparations for supper.

But neither grandparent was in the kitchen or dining room. Muffled voices sounded from the direction of the parlor, and Emily wondered who was paying a call at this time of night. Maybe the new preacher had arrived sooner than expected. She held her breath and without removing her wraps, tiptoed down the hall.

There were no guests, but a tree was in a stand, its lofty branches filling one corner of the room. Emily stood, staring in disbelief.

"Surprise!" Grandfather called out. "Come see what we have done."

Stringed popcorn and tiny candles decorated the Douglas fir, and she recognized it as one of the trees from the corner of the acreage. Each year in the past Emily deco-

rated a tree with material scraps and bits of colored yarn.
When one grew too tall, she found a smaller one. She had
asked to bring a tree into the house that first year she came
to Oregon. They always had one in California and it was
just one small part she missed, but when she asked her
grandmother about it, she scoffed, saying they didn't have
time for such foolishness on the farm.

"Any size would do," she remembered begging those first
years. But they had been adamant, especially Grandmother.
And Grandfather always went along because it was easier.
Yet Emily thought she caught a glimpse of empathy from
him. If it was up to him, he would have said, "Fine, let's
cut a tree." Now she had her tree, and she wondered at his
decision. She knew it was Grandfather who had taken
special effort to go chop the tree, then haul it to the house.
Chores were difficult to do, so this took extra work and
time. How had this come about when Grandmother always
claimed it was pure nonsense and in no way honored the
Christ Child? It was the same reason Grandmother gave
when Emily wanted to cut and bring in a bouquet of spring
blossoms. "They look much prettier outside. That's where
God intended them to be."

Emily's first few years on the farm had been magical
with the forest of trees, their branches forming a canopy
over her head when she went on evening walks in the sum-
mer. Then as the need arose, Grandfather sold off the tim-
ber, then the lot, then more trees, until the only ones left
were the few bordering their property. Emily's trees had
been on the line. She was surprised Grandfather had cut
one.

She clasped her hands, still saying nothing.

"Well, what does thee think?" Grandmother stood back,
hands on hips. "It was your grandfather's idea, of course.

He wanted to surprise thee."

"And it looks as if we've succeeded," Grandfather said. "Yes, thee is certainly surprised."

Emily took a deep breath. The tree, perfectly round, sat in the corner by the window, its fragrance filling the parlor that usually smelled musty. The window faced east, and that was why they hadn't seen Emily trudging up the lane after hopping out of Ben's carriage. Looking at the decorated tree, at her grandparents, she burst into tears before fleeing from the room.

She heard the sound of her grandparents' voices echoing as they came down the hall. Grabbing the bucket, she ran outside to pump water. Pumping water gave her time to think. It was a day of surprises. The tree made her happy. Seeing Ben made her happy, so why was she acting in this strange way? Why was she crying now? Wiping her tears on the sleeve of the threadbare dark coat, she pumped all the harder. Soon the bucket was full and coming down over the side, wetting her feet. She stopped, jumping back, noticing the small puddle.

The back door opened and Grandmother stood, as if waiting for an answer, an explanation for Emily's unexpected outburst. Emily took a deep breath and lifted the bucket up, and moved past Grandmother who had not spoken. The light from the lamp cast shadows on the dishes, as she hoisted the bucket up onto the small wash stand. The table was set, as it always was, while they waited for her return from work. She smelled the savory aroma of beef stew bubbling at the back of the stove. Big chunks of bread filled the plate, while butter and homemade cherry preserves sat in the middle of the table.

"Now, what was the reason for thy tears?" Grandmother wasn't about to let it go. "You asked for a tree, and now you have one. It was too tall for the ceiling, so your grandfather had to chop off the trunk, then make a stand."

Her grandfather hobbled into the kitchen, regarding her curiously. "Thy cheeks do look unusually bright—"

"A dose of cod liver oil is what thee needs."

"The tree. . .it's lovely," Emily finally said. "I. . .I was crying happy tears, not sad ones."

"Happy tears? Never heard of such!" Grandmother scoffed.

"Yes, thee has," Grandfather remarked. "Thee cried on our wedding day. Now tell me, were those tears of happiness or sadness?"

Grandmother "humphed," and turned her back. Seconds later, the stew filled a bowl, the steam rising to the ceiling. "I say it's time to eat."

They sat and silently asked the blessing.

Emily sat rigid, her eyes filling again. She couldn't explain it. Perhaps it was guilt. Guilt for going to the dance. Guilt for riding home with Ben. Guilt for her transgressions. And then to come in to find the tree, a tree so beautiful it took her breath away. The shock was too much.

"Perhaps thee would like to add the paper chains to the tree after supper," Grandmother said, passing the stew to Emily.

"I didn't know thee saved them." Emily had been surprised to see them in a box, and even more surprised to hear herself lapse into the old speech.

"Yes, I did."

Later they sat in the parlor instead of by the fire. Emily had placed the red and green paper chains around the tree, adding the touch it needed. It was the most beautiful sight she had ever seen. The fragrance filled her being with its piney scent and she wanted the moment to last forever.

"Thee had a good idea," Grandfather said then. "I wish we'd had a tree before this."

They settled against the cushions as Emily read Luke's version of the Christmas story. "And there were in the same country shepherds abiding in the field keeping watch over their flock by night. And lo, the angel of the Lord came upon them, and the glory of the Lord shone round about them and they were sore afraid."

"We are having tea before the prayers," Grandmother said then. "A cup of tea, prayers, and then to bed."

But Emily sat in the parlor long after Grandmother removed the lamp. She wanted to smell the pine, think her thoughts, say her prayers. Things were changing, and it frightened her. It all began with that dance. And somehow she couldn't imagine how that could have anything to do with it. Yet it seemed to. At the thought of Ben, she trembled, thinking how wonderful it had been to ride in his carriage. Studying the side of his face, that wild thatch of hair, watching the way he held the reins, the gentle way he commanded the horses to "gee" when it was time to trot.

When he had held her arm as she climbed up, before leaving the candy factory, she had looked just once into his eyes. The same look was there and even now she could see it. It made her cheeks come afire at the memory.

Emily wished she could go riding in Ben's fine carriage some evening. She wished he could come in and see the decorated tree and have a cup of tea with her and the grandparents. She also wished he might come to meeting, that he believed as she did. But if "wishes were horses, beggars might ride," Grandmother always said.

She finally rose to her feet, fetched the lamp by the stove, the one Grandmother always left burning for her. Its flame burned low so as to save kerosene. Even in the stairway she could smell the tree's piney fragrance. It was going to be a wonderful Christmas after all. The most wonderful one she could remember since coming to Oregon.

six

Emily could hardly wait to tell Kate about the Christmas tree the next day. She was also eager to give her the gift she'd made, knowing Kate would exclaim over the muffler even if she didn't wear black.

It was Tuesday, the day before Christmas. They would work all day, filling the last minute orders for Oregon's Finest Chocolates, but they had Christmas and the next day off.

"Well, you're certainly looking happy," Kate said moments after removing her coat. "Almost as good as the night of the dance."

Emily's smile faded.

"Oh, oh, sorry I mentioned it. What happened?"

Emily told her about the tree and about drinking tea in the parlor.

"Maybe they suddenly realized how much they depend on you, and how little you ask for," Kate said. "I've been praying for you, Emily. Praying we'll find a way to get you to California. I just wanted you to know that."

Emily felt a warm glow as she thought about Kate praying for her. Imagine that. It was a good thing she had that to think about because they were so busy filling orders, they cut their dinner time in half. One of the orders had come from Ben. He wanted an assortment of bonbons, and insisted that Emily be the one to make the candy. Now as she placed the sweet confections in the small box, she wondered who was going to receive the gift. Not that it was any concern of hers.

Mr. Roberts, pleased with all the last minute orders, apologized for keeping the girls overtime. "Once the holidays are over, we'll be back to normal working hours."

Emily thought about the box of bonbons several times. Imagine Ben asking her to make them. Imagine Kate praying for her, understanding Emily's need to see her family again. Imagine a tree in the house. Imagine Ben taking her home. Imagine a man looking at her in that way—the way that made her toes all tingly.

"Ben has his train tickets for Iowa," Kate said as they left for the dinner break. "He talked about it while taking me home last night."

"So that's who gets the candy."

"He says he will bring his mother and sister back after he sells the farm."

"He won't be back."

"Yes, he will," Kate insisted. "His mother was widowed last year, and he promised his father before he died that he would look out for her and his little sister."

This promise to his father proved he was a man of his word, Emily thought. Yes, duty prevails. Hadn't she done her duty, too?

"He is coming by tonight," Kate said, biting into a celery chunk. "I'm sure it's because he wants to see you again."

Emily shrugged. He had said something about it, but she hadn't believed him, nor had she encouraged him. She wanted to, how she wanted to, but to do so was wrong, especially when she knew they could never plan a life together.

"I can't have him calling, Kate. You've got to understand why."

"Well, I don't understand why, Emily. Truly you should encourage him. He's a fine man and worthy of you. He's not only intelligent, but has a bright future. There's a demand for good builders in Oregon, and he does wonderful work."

Emily wrapped the remains of her sandwich and said nothing. Then she remembered Kate's gift. They'd been so busy, she'd all but forgotten it.

"I brought you a small Christmas present."

Kate smiled. "I have something for you, also. I didn't mention it before, because I didn't know how you felt about receiving gifts from friends. Let's open them now. Why wait until tomorrow?" Kate said, bringing out a small package wrapped in pale green paper. "Besides, I want to see what you think."

Emily's eyes widened at the beautiful paper. "Kate, I cannot open this. It's too pretty."

"Silly," Kate said. "Go on. It's only paper."

Slowly, meticulously, Emily unwrapped her present, careful not to tear the paper. A silver hair clasp with a scroll design shone under the light. "Oh, Kate, it's the most beautiful thing I've ever seen."

Kate grabbed Emily's braids, unwound them and pinned the braids together so they fell down her back. "It would go nice like this."

Emily couldn't see how it looked, but she knew it must look elegant. Not that she could wear it to church or around her grandparents, but it was a lovely gift, something she would keep forever.

"Thank you so much, Kate." The words barely escaped past the lump in her throat. "I'll cherish it always." She paused for a long moment. "And here's your gift." She handed Kate the clumsily wrapped present in plain brown paper.

Kate unwrapped the oblong package and exclaimed loudly when she saw the muffler. "Emily, it's wonderful! It's just what I need." She wrapped it around her neck and held her head high. "I truly mean it. It's so warm. And to think you knit it."

"It isn't your color—"

"Maybe not, but it's a good, neutral color, and will go with everything I own." She leaned over and hugged Emily hard. "I will wear it proudly."

The women went back to work and Emily kept thinking about the silver clasp, thinking how lovely it was. She was so lucky to have a friend like Kate.

She thought about Ben the rest of the afternoon. What would she say to him? *Hurry back to Oregon?* No. She couldn't encourage him when she knew it wouldn't work. He didn't believe as she did and that was her main concern. The new preacher coming was the one God had in mind for her. It had to be; the timing was right. Emily and he would have a mutual love of the Lord. Together they would pray for the Meeting and be good citizens in the community. How could she ask or hope for more?

Ben was punctual. It was five-thirty and Emily had finished his order. He walked to the cloakroom where both women were putting on their wraps.

"May I give you a ride home?" His eyes fastened on Emily with an expectant look.

"I'm not going tonight because Kurt is coming in a few minutes," Kate replied.

"I don't mean to be rude," Emily said, her eyes avoiding Ben's, "but I cannot ride with you. It isn't right."

Ben doffed his hat. "I'm trying to understand, Emily. Kate has explained a few things—about your grandparents."

"There's more," Emily said, not wanting to go into it now. Besides, he wouldn't agree.

"I'll be leaving the day after tomorrow."

"Kate mentioned it."

"I wanted to talk. . .to tell you about my plans. . .to see what you thought. . ."

Emily's breath caught in her throat. Why would Ben want to tell her about his plans? Why would he care what she thought?

"I. . ." the words had difficulty getting out. "I can't see you, Ben. We are too different—"

"Different," he repeated. "But that can be good."

"Not when it comes to honoring God—"

"I see." He turned and without another word walked toward the door. She saw the slump of his shoulders, the way he looked down, and she felt a sudden emptiness. Tears sprang to her eyes. Why was she feeling this way? How could this be happening to her? She knew in that instant that she must talk to Ben again—that she couldn't shut him out of her life. That she didn't want to, though her brain said, yes, yes, it's the only way.

"Ben. . ." It was but a whisper, but he heard and turned.

"Yes, Emily?"

"I would like a ride after all."

He walked back and tucked her hand under his arm.

Kate had wrapped the muffler around her neck and smiled. "Merry Christmas, you two. I'll see you on Friday, Emily. Goodnight, Ben. And do have a good trip." She leaned over, hugging Emily, then headed for the door.

"I'll see you when I return," he called after Kate.

Before assisting her into the buggy, Ben handed Emily two lumps of sugar. "Thought you might like to feed the horses."

Emily laughed as each horse took his sugar and shook his head as if to say thank you.

Ben made sure she was comfortable before taking the reins. "I'm glad you changed your mind since I may not see you again."

"Kate said you were returning to Iowa the day after Christmas."

He nodded, and she liked the way his chin jutted out. He wore a proud look, one of confidence. Her heart pounded harder than before. It hardly seemed possible that she could be riding with a man in one of the most beautiful carriages she had ever seen. And to think it was his idea— his desire to have her ride with him.

The horses settled down to a slower gait.

"I must convince my mother how beautiful Oregon is. Pearl—my little sister—is ready to come. Together we'll work on Ma."

"And then when I get back. . ." He let the reins fall and the horses stopped. "Emily, I want to come calling when I return. Whatever it takes. If I need to speak to your grandparents, that's fine. I will do that. I will attend your church. Study the doctrine. I am willing to do what is necessary."

She looked away from his intense gaze. How she longed to have him touch her, to pull her into his arms, but of course it wouldn't be right. She mustn't think like this.

He turned her face toward his with his gloved hand. He had to look into those eyes, the eyes he could read so well. Ben knew how Emily felt about him, even without the words, it was there, written on her face, shining in her eyes. If only she could understand it was meant to be.

She raised a hand to her face and looked away. "I have been promised to another man. Remember I spoke of him the night of the dance."

His eyes blazed. "Kate says you haven't even met this man."

"I know, but he is of my faith. He's a good man who lost his wife and baby. He needs a wife."

"Emily," he took her small hand and held it tight. "All I ask is a chance for you to get to know me, and me to know you."

Emily said nothing, knowing it was hopeless. Ben could meet her grandparents. He could promise to honor God, to be part of the Friends' Meeting, but he would be doing it for the wrong reasons. It would never be acceptable.

"I can't give you that chance," Emily finally said.

He nodded, his eyes looked straight ahead. "I thought you would say that."

How could he tell her he wanted to change, to go along with the precepts of her church? That his faith was strong and powerful. Because he was of no particular denomination did not mean he didn't love God, or that he didn't serve Him. He did, it was just in a different way. He couldn't believe that God had let Emily cross his path, only to have her taken away to marry someone she hadn't even met, someone who was marrying her because he needed a wife, not because he loved her.

His hand felt the gift in his pocket. Should he give it to her now, or would he wait until after the next church service? He could put off the trip for a few days. All he knew was that it was impossible for him to leave her like this, knowing he didn't have any kind of a chance.

"Emily, I want to see you once more before I go east. I *must* see you again. I'll be at church Wednesday evening."

Her cheeks flamed at the thought. "No, Ben. Go to your family. That's what God would have you do."

"God also wants me to have a wife. I've prayed for one

for a good long while and believe that it is you."

Emily didn't know how to respond to Ben's declaration.

The horses started to canter and a wintry breeze blew into the open carriage. She didn't want to go home. She wanted to stay here forever, to feel Ben's strong presence, to go with him wherever he went, even if it was to Iowa. But she knew it wasn't possible. It wasn't right. The time to say good-bye had come. She must not see him again.

The house came into view and she laid a hand on Ben's coat. "Please, stop now. I must go in. I am already quite late."

He stopped the carriage and again she hopped down before he could help her.

"Emily, think about what I said."

She nodded and hurried off, not daring to look back. She wanted to see his face once more, to look into those eyes, to feel him beside her in the carriage, but it was over. She had to return to the life she had known. Another man was on the horizon—a man who was more like her, and would be acceptable to her grandparents, to the Friends.

He watched until she disappeared into a house at the end of the rutted road. It was partially concealed by naked maple trees. He wanted to go after her, to touch her again, to lift her eyes to meet his. Even more he wanted to touch her lips, but knew he couldn't. Not now. Not yet.

He shivered from the early evening breeze and picked up the reins. He *would* see her again. Just once more before he left for Iowa. It wasn't a case of "want to" but a case of have to.

seven

Emily didn't look back once, though she knew Ben stayed at the corner, watching her, waiting for her to go inside. She hoped Grandmother wouldn't notice her pink cheeks. Walking in the winter, though it was only ten blocks from the streetcar stop, usually made her cheeks red, and especially so when it was windy.

When she stepped inside, she smelled the fragrant pine and it made her heart even lighter. Grandmother was already dishing up supper, so she washed up and slipped into her chair.

"I will certainly be glad when Christmas is over," Grandmother said, "so thee can back to a regular time of getting home."

Supper was eaten, the wood gathered, water pumped, and the dishes washed, rinsed, and left to drain on the sideboard.

Prayers and Bible reading were said in the parlor again that night. The tree seemed to glow from the corner and filled Emily with such gladness, she could scarcely believe it. That, along with the memories of Ben raced through her mind, making her feel warm and good. She wondered if he really would come to the Wednesday night Christmas meeting, or would he be too busy with his upcoming trip?

She read the scripture from Matthew where it spoke of praying together: . . .*where two or three are gathered together in my name, there I am.* . . She wondered if Ben was saying the same prayer she was. *Let there be a way,*

God. Oh, let there be a way. . .

Her thoughts surprised her, tormented her. Even as she prayed, down deep she knew to hope was wrong. God answered prayers; it just wasn't always the way one wanted.

The extra work had made her tired, but for some reason she could not sleep, not even after writing in her diary. Ben's face, his eyes kept crowding her thoughts. If only she hadn't met him. How much less complicated life would be now.

She held the silver clasp in her hand before placing it in the night stand drawer. She wanted to wear it again, but knew Grandmother wouldn't approve.

&

Christmas morning Emily woke to the sound of a gentle rain hitting the roof. No sunshine for the special day. It was okay. She didn't need to go to work. They would eat breakfast, she'd hurry through the chores, and then it would be time to open the few gifts they had made for each other. Grandfather's gift had been the Christmas tree, and perhaps that was part of Grandmother's, too. It was more than she ever dreamed for. She had already received one special gift—Kate's.

"Merry Christmas, Emily," Grandfather called, smiling over his cup of coffee. "May the Lord our God bless thee richly this day."

Emily leaned over, hugging her grandfather. Grandmother turned from the stove, placing a bowl of steaming oats in front of her husband.

"Christmas is like any other day. I can't understand the fuss."

"Thee makes presents every year," Grandfather said, a twinkle in his eye.

"That's because thee makes something for me."

Soon they were in the parlor and Emily looked at her beautiful tree. She handed Grandfather his present.

"Wool socks. Just what I needed." He looked at them with admiration. "You do a better job every year."

"Humph!" Grandmother scowled as she opened her gift from Emily. "Tea towels. Thee does know what I need."

Grandfather gave Emily a decoration for the tree. He had painted a face on a walnut shell, adding cat fur for hair. She placed it on the tree, close to the top. Next was the gift from Grandmother. A black knit hat that covered her ears and had ties. Emily put it on, liking the warmth of the wool.

"Thank you so much." She leaned over and hugged Grandfather, then Grandmother. Her grandmother, not used to such displays of affection, pulled away.

"I'd like to hear some Scripture," she said.

"But thee didn't open my gift," Grandfather said, handing over a bulky looking parcel.

"Oh. Thee shouldn't have."

Grandmother said that every year, too.

A straw basket was under the wrappings and Grandmother actually smiled. "Where did thee find a basket like this?"

"At the emporium that last time we went. I thought thee might like it for thy dried flowers."

Emily read the Christmas story from Matthew and they had prayers. The day flew by quickly and at last it was time for the evening meeting. The rain had stopped and Emily smelled deeply of the night air. Would Ben come? She tried not to think about it, but he kept slipping into her thoughts.

❧

She started the evening meeting with a medly of Christmas

carols.

Emily sang as she played, wishing the carols could be played more often than once a year. She had begun the third verse of "Angels from the Realms of Glory" when the outer door opened. She felt the whoosh of cold night air blowing in, and turned half way to see Ben Galloway taking off his hat as he stepped inside. Her heart nearly stopped as one of her fingers hit a wrong key.

He had come, as he said he would. She felt her cheeks flush as she continued the song, chiding herself for trembling inside. How could she have doubted his word? Though she knew very little about him, she knew he was a man of promise. He was also a man of determination, and she couldn't help but wonder what people were thinking as this tall, handsome stranger entered their midst. Would they believe he had just come to worship? It didn't matter. The Society of Friends was open to anyone coming who needed prayer and uplifting.

When the hymn was over, Emily stood and walked over to her usual pew. She could feel Ben's eyes on her, watching, but she didn't dare glance in his direction to acknowledge his presence. She wondered what he would think of the meeting. Surely this was different than other church services he had attended. Most churches did not have long, silent prayers during the service.

Emily's prayer was for a quiet heart, a calm spirit, but neither happened. After the end of the meeting, she rushed to the back of the room.

Ben waited just outside the door. He tipped his hat and smiled. "I had to see you tonight since my train leaves at six in the morning."

"I. . .pray for a safe trip for thee."

"Thank you." His eyes fastened on her. "I enjoyed your

playing. It was beautiful and reminded me of my sister Anna. She plays piano and violin."

His voice glowed as he spoke of his sister and Emily felt herself relax for a moment. "My father used to play the violin when I was little. I'd go to sleep listening to 'Arkansas Traveler.' He came from Arkansas." A lump came to her throat at the memory.

"Come. Can we talk over there by my buggy where everyone can see us, but perhaps not hear us?"

"Let me tell my grandparents where I am—"

But she need not have bothered as everyone's eyes were on Ben. Dressed in tweeds and brown felt hat, he stood out from the others in their simple, plain dress.

Emily saw Grandmother watching her, so she pointed toward Ben's carriage.

"Thee must not take too long," Grandmother said, her voice full of disapproval.

Ben was stroking the neck of one of the horses when Emily walked up.

"It was a nice prayer meeting, Emily. I'm very glad I came."

"I'm glad you came, too." And she meant it, though she knew he was too worldly, and the Friends would never approve. If he had been a Methodist or a Nazarene, he might have been accepted, but not to belong to any church was unthinkable.

"I don't know how long I'll be gone, Emily," he said, his eyes holding hers. "It depends on Ma and the farm and how fast I can sell it. There are many factors."

"I understand."

He took her hand for a brief moment. "I want you to remember what I said yesterday. I meant it. Every word. My heart knows what it wants and needs, and I must see you when I return."

She trembled at his words, wanting to say something, yet knowing she couldn't trust her voice to speak. Must. He had said he *must* see her again.

"You spoke of a man last night. Is he here?"

Luke. He was referring to Luke. She shook her head. "He's due to arrive next week."

A frown creased Ben's forehead. The timing couldn't be more wrong. Here he was leaving, and it was taking all he could muster to do that, and another man was entering Emily's life. A godly man. A preacher. One of whom she would approve, one whom her grandparents and the others would deem worthy and right for her. If ever there was a God—which Ben believed with all his heart—he needed Him on his side like never before. How could he possibly win her over? The competition was unfair. Though Ben had never had a problem convincing a woman of his intentions, this was different. This time it was for real. He wanted her more than anything he had ever wanted.

"When I return I hope to meet this man." He moved closer. "Pray for me, Emily. I need your prayers. I so admire your strong faith."

"I don't think—"

"No, wait. Let me finish." His hand reached out, then stopped. "I will go to your church, Emily Drake, if that's what it takes. I will worship God in the way you do, if that's what it takes. I truly meant what I said last night. I will do whatever it takes—"

"You must worship God because you want to," Emily said then, "not because you think someone expects it. Wanting to is what's important, what counts."

"I worship God now. Always have. My mother taught me prayers and songs from the time I was knee high." He shook his head. "Did you think I was a heathen? That I don't serve God because I dance? That's the real problem, isn't it, Emily?"

Her breath seemed to catch under her rib cage. What could she say? How could she explain that it was the dancing that set him apart from others who believed? How could she discourage this man, who thought it was okay to dance? Even though he believed, which was admirable, it wouldn't be right because he was not of her persuasion.

"Emily, we are leaving."

"I must go," she said as her grandparents' wagon approached. Already she wondered what they would say. There would be countless questions and she would probably end up telling them how she met Ben.

"I can give up dancing," he said then. "It isn't a problem for me."

"You don't know our doctrine—"

"I will learn it then."

"Emily!" the voice was sharper this time.

"I have to go—"

"Emily. . ." His hand reached out. "I will see you again. And that's a promise." He stepped in front, blocking the view of her. Looking down, his dark eyes met hers, and before she could tear away from that penetrating gaze, he leaned over and brushed his lips against her cheek.

"This is for you," he said, pressing a small object into her gloved hand. "A Christmas present. I've been working on it all week long."

"But," she started to protest, "I can't possibly take—"

"It's a gift," he said. "Of course you can take it."

"But. . .I. . .it's wrong to accept a gift."

"I want you to have it to remember me by."

Without saying another word, he jumped onto the buggy

seat and shook the reins.

Emily's face, hot from his touch, stood as if suspended in space. Her heart soared as she watched through the darkened shadows at Ben Galloway's retreating back, riding off into the dark night. She unclasped the hard object, and held it out in front of her. It was a tiny horse carved from wood. It was beautiful, the hard wood soft and smooth. For her. A gift for her. And he had made it. She swallowed hard as she tucked it into the pocket of her winter coat.

He would be gone first thing in the morning and she wondered if she would ever see him again. He said he would return, but would he? Iowa was a long way from Oregon. There were extenuating circumstances. Ben's mother. A sister. Perhaps they wouldn't want to move out West. Perhaps they would talk Ben into staying there.

I'll wait, an inner voice said. *Yes, I will wait, though I know I shouldn't. Though I know it means trouble, I will wait.*

Turning, she walked to the wagon, bracing herself for the words she knew were coming, the lectures, the prayers, and the "how could you even dare think?"

The night sky had never looked so illuminated or so full of stars. And though Emily did not believe in signs, she knew one when she saw it. This was a sign from God that someone cared for her deeply. And she cared back. There was no denying it any longer. And even if he didn't come back, just knowing that he thought enough of her to carve a gift, to come to meeting so he could see her one last time, to kiss her cheek was almost more than she could stand.

eight

Emily ran to the wagon and hoisting her skirts up, climbed in. She could feel several pairs of eyes on her, watching, wondering. She wanted to look back to see if she could still see Ben and his carriage, but kept her eyes staring straight ahead. Her heart pounded in her ears as her fingers traced the spot on her cheek where he had kissed her. It had been a gentle kiss, a kiss of promise. It was also the first kiss she had ever received. She knew without asking that her grandparents would never allow her to be courted by someone who didn't belong to the meeting.

They wouldn't get two blocks, she knew, before Grandmother began questioning.

It was one block.

"Who was that man?"

She felt the color rush to her cheeks again.

"Thee knows him from where?" Grandfather asked, before Emily could answer.

"He's Kate's friend," she finally said

"Thee saw him that night thee stayed there."

"Yes."

"Why would he come to meeting?" Grandmother asked.

"He wanted to say good-bye."

"Good-bye?" The grandparents' voices echoed in unison.

"He is returning to Iowa where his mother and sister live. His name is Ben Galloway." Her fingers tightened around the tiny horse in her pocket. The wood was stained

73

a beautiful ebony color so that it resembled his new team of horses.

"When did thee meet him?" Grandmother was persistent.

"Kate introduced us."

Grandmother clicked her tongue. "I knew thee shouldn't go over there that night."

"He's a very nice person," Emily said in his defense.

"But not of our faith." Grandmother drew her wraps closer to ward off the chilly night air.

"No, not of our faith," Grandfather repeated.

"He believes in God. He told me so himself."

"Thee seems to know a lot about him already."

"He came to the factory. We talked there."

It was true. He had come and they had talked. Of course he had taken her home, but she didn't mention that. Still, she had not lied. Every word was true. She just hadn't embellished on it.

"I don't know much. I think he works with wood, building things, like cabinets." Her hand squeezed the small horse.

"Why is he in Oregon?"

"He came with a brother, I believe Kate said."

"Is he returning?"

"He might. He does work for the Talbot family."

Grandfather raised his eyebrows. "They must have paid him well. That would explain the fancy carriage and fine team of horses."

"Yes, I guess so—" Emily said under her breath.

"What else does thee know about him?" Grandmother wasn't through interrogating.

"He leaves for Iowa on the morning train. There. You don't need to be concerned anymore."

"Don't thee use that tone of voice with me," Grandmother

said, squaring her shoulders in that formidable way that always frightened Emily.

"I'm sorry." Emily looked away.

"Thee hasn't forgotten about Pastor Morrison?"

"No." And she hadn't. She knew he would be far the better choice, yet there was something about Ben that wouldn't let her mind, or her heart, let go. The night air was cold, but Emily felt warm inside. Her heart pounded and everything inside her seemed to be whirling around and around crazily.

"He isn't right for thee," Grandfather said, giving the horses an extra coaxing with the reins.

"I should certainly say not," Grandmother added. "Did thee see the expensive suit he wore? Obviously he's of the world and doesn't believe in charitable offerings."

"I think it is his brother's suit."

"And that hat. New and fancy. Must have cost a tidy sum," Grandfather went on, seemingly not hearing Emily's comment about the suit.

"We lead a simple life, as you always have, Emily. You cannot put your trust in someone like that," Grandmother went on.

"He is just an acquaintance," Emily repeated.

"Thee would not be happy to be courted by someone who did not believe as thee does," Grandfather said.

They were at the end of the lane and Emily remembered the two rides from Ben. How she had hoped he could come in, to meet her grandparents, see the Christmas tree, sit and have a cup of tea, but he wouldn't have been welcome. They would never accept him, no matter if he did believe in God. He wasn't a Friend. He would never fit in. Kate didn't understand, nor did Ben, but that was the way things were.

"Pastor Morrison arrives next Saturday. All the way

from Ohio," Beulah announced, just as Grandfather called the horses to halt. "Myrtle Lee received a letter, and the time of his arrival."

"We will invite him for Sunday dinner," Grandfather said. Seems fitting, don't you think?"

Grandmother nodded as she climbed down from the wagon. "I imagine he won't go wanting for food for the first few weeks."

It would seem strange, Emily thought, to have a preacher presiding over the meetings. She could never remember that happening before. It might be nice for a change, but what might not be so nice were the expectations directed toward her. Maybe she would have no feeling toward him. What then?

The grandparents went into the house and moments later Emily saw the soft glow from the lamps. She lingered outside, gazing at the canopy of stars overhead. The clear, dark sky promised a nice day, one without rain. *A good traveling day for Ben.* She prayed for a safe trip, and that his thoughts might be of her, even if nothing could ever develop between them. Her fingers closed around the tiny horse in her pocket. She would keep it always in memory of the tall man with thick, bushy hair and eyebrows to match.

Emily opened the door, remembering her forgotten chores. It was a wonder that Grandmother hadn't reminded her. "I'm getting the water and wood," she said, slipping out the back door before removing her wraps.

She was thankful now that she'd chopped so much wood the night before. A bit of kindling, a few large chunks, and two buckets of water should do.

The lamp burned low on the kitchen table, giving Emily enough light to see the water stand. She poured cold water into the basin to wash her face and hands in preparation for bed. The icy water felt good on her hot cheeks. She felt the spot gingerly where Ben's lips had touched so briefly.

"Emily!"

She jumped. "Yes, Grandmother?"

"Thee better go to bed now. We will talk more about this situation tomorrow."

"Yes, Grandmother."

She watched as Grandmother went down the hall carrying a lamp. It was time for bed and she should have been tired, but surprisingly she felt light-headed. Awake. Alert.

The house was quiet as Emily sat in semi-darkness at the kitchen table. Had Ben really meant that he wanted her to wait for him? Would it be acceptable if he were to be dedicated in meeting? Would he then be permitted to come calling? No, she told herself. Why did she think one way one minute, then change her mind? What was wrong with her? How could she have even considered waiting? It wasn't meant to be. How could she dare hope?

Emily paused in the doorway of the parlor, breathing in the scent of the Christmas tree. Ben would be home shortly after Christmas, surrounded by loved ones. She wondered what sort of celebration they would have. She also wondered what his mother looked like and if she was a hugging type person, or if she was more austere like Grandmother. Somehow, she didn't think so. Ben was not standoffish. She could imagine him taking her into his arms and kissing her on the lips. If the Friends hadn't been milling about in the meetinghouse's yard, he might have done that very thing tonight. She would have acted shocked, of course, and he might have apologized. As it was, her first kiss on the cheek was one she would remember for the rest of her life.

She looked at the tree one last time, took the lamp and

proceeded up the steps. She'd left her coat on the hook, but in her right hand was the horse. He was so smooth, so finely carved, from the tip of his head to his tail. The mane was free flowing with ears sharp and pointed. He looked like Ben's horses. Proud as they pranced, heads held high. Her horse might be a race horse with legs that galloped. Free. Oh, to be free like her horse. Free to make decisions. She wondered when Ben had learned to whittle. The horse was something she would always cherish and keep hidden in a drawer beside her bed.

Had she thanked Ben properly for his gift? She'd been so surprised, she didn't think she'd said anything. It wasn't right to accept the horse since she hadn't given him a gift. If only she had knit him a pair of socks. But she didn't know the size of his feet. Closing her eyes, she remembered looking at them the night they had waltzed. They weren't large, nor were they small. Just about average, she decided. Maybe she could guess. Maybe she could work on a pair of socks during dinner at work. If she knit at home, Grandmother would ask questions.

She set the horse on the night stand next to her Bible and diary. It was her fourth treasure. Besides the diary, a picture brother Tommy had drawn after she moved to Oregon, the silver hair clasp, and now the horse.

The horse needed a name. She thought about Black Beauty after the book she had heard in fourth grade class. Or Belle, after Grandfather's old nag. Ben's team of horses didn't have names, or none that she knew of.

"Black Beauty," she said aloud, and picking it up once more, she held it close to her heart for a long moment. It was the last thing she saw before slipping off to sleep for the night. . .

nine

Ben Galloway had never felt so alone as he did that night after leaving Emily in the churchyard. Standing there with her hands folded, her eyes watching him, he had wanted to go back, take her into his arms and kiss her full on the lips. Her cheek felt soft, and he knew his brief kiss had surprised her. Since he had moved in front of her, covering her with his bulk, her grandparents would not have seen anything to construe all wrong. Surely there was nothing wrong with a kiss on the cheek, but from all indications, they were over-protective.

He knew Emily cared for him. The expression in her eyes told all. He now dreaded the trip back to Iowa, wondering how he would manage without her. Her smile would be in his mind, the touch of her hand, the imagined feel of her small, fragile frame.

Would he be able to speed up things? Convince his mother she should sell the homestead and come back with him to Oregon?

And when was this preacher fellow arriving? What if Emily succumbed to his charm? What if he promised to love and cherish her? Since he served the Friends and believed as Emily did, he might win her over, and would definitely convince the grandparents.

Even as he thought it, his hands tightening on the reins, he knew she couldn't love this man as she loved him. It was an unselfish love, for he had it figured out that Emily wouldn't know how to be selfish. It was not something she had learned living with her grandparents. Ben had been selfish when he left Ma and Pearl alone on the farm. Jesse had always been selfish, doing what he wanted, not helping with the farm, nor working with Pa in his wood shop. Jesse fished, hunted, and later drove into town and met women. He never told Ma or Pa, never bragged about his conquests, but Ben knew they knew. They chose to ignore it in the stoic way of the Scots.

Ben's selfish days were past. He now had someone to live for. Someone to pour his heart out to. He had never felt that way before. Was this what it was all about? Could this be the way Pa felt about Ma when he saw her at the edge of the creek bank wading in the water that hot, July afternoon? He knew his parents had cared deeply for each other. Ma had borne seven babies. All had lived. All healthy. She was a raw-boned woman and it was from that Ben acquired his broadness, his height. Pa had been of slighter build, though tall and angular. He had not worked the land. That had been Ma and the kids' job. And Ma loved the land. Loved growing vegetables. How she would delight in the rich, black earth of the Willamette Valley. He could picture her now, bent over her hoe, breaking up the clods, preparing the ground for spring planting.

Ben had not received this love for working the land, but instead thrilled at the aspect of what one could do with a good piece of wood. Cabinets. Tables and chairs, were all things he had learned by watching his father measure carefully, then cut. He had taught Ben to whittle, how to use wood, how to be proud of a chest of drawers, a rocking chair, a set of shelves. There had always been a demand for Jebediah Galloway's work, and he'd built things right up until he took so sick he couldn't hold his head up. Pneumonia, the doctor said. Aggravated by daily breathing sawdust. Whatever, it was wicked and Ben watched as his father grew thinner. Weaker. He seemed to die right before his eyes and there wasn't a thing the doctor or anyone could do.

Jesse had gone off somewhere and didn't even know his Pa was ailing, didn't even know when he died, because he hadn't sent an address or been in touch. He showed up six months after Pa was buried.

"Ben, you gotta come back with me."

"Where to?"

"Oregon. It's great land out there." Jesse's dark eyes glistened with unusual brightness. "Businesses are springing up all over and any man who can do an honest day's work can make money."

Ma had sat, her lips pressed tight. Ben knew what she was thinking. When Ma was angry she got quiet. She was far too quiet now.

"Ma, come with us," Ben urged. "We'll build a new home."

She refused to budge. "I'll be fine right here. This is home. This way I can go to the graveyard every day and talk to your Pa. That's the way it's got to be."

Pearl at fourteen, with waist-length thick, dark hair, begged her mother to go. "Ma, there's nothing to stay here for now. Let's go." But even as she pleaded, she knew it wouldn't work. And being the youngest, her job was to stay here with Ma. That was just the way it was.

Jesse waited a week, working on Ben until he finally agreed to go. On a temporary basis.

"I'm leaving you in charge," Ben said, lifting Pearl's dark blue eyes to meet his gaze. "Here's some money to take care of you, and there are plenty of supplies until I return. I'll be back for you, and if it's as Jesse says, I won't take no for an answer. I have to be the 'man of the family' with Pa gone and Ma is going to have to come."

"How long will you be gone, Benjamin?"

Ma stood behind him, her hands folded across her ample bosom. She didn't like the conversation she'd just heard and told Ben so.

"Ma, if I can make a better living, then that's what I must do. I'm not a farmer. I can't be. I want to build things like Pa did. Please try to understand."

The train trip had been difficult. Jesse was raging with a sudden fever and just when Ben had decided to take him off at the next stop to see a doctor—they were somewhere in Montana—Jesse pulled through.

He was involved in a poker game the following day and lost all his money to a rich widow from Eureka, California.

Jesse stayed with the widow and went to Seattle, leaving his clothes with Ben, while Ben got off the train in Spokane, and headed on to Portland.

The beauty of the land as the train passed through the Columbia River Gorge surpassed his wildest imagination and he was hooked. Immense fir trees seemed to touch the sky. The Columbia was as long as he could see. He heard it didn't stop until it reached the Pacific Ocean.

At his first glimpse of the Willamette River, Ben lifted his face skyward. He didn't pray with his eyes closed, but always looked up, as if he could see his Maker.

"God, I know this is where You want me to be. What a beautiful spot!"

It was time to settle down, and Jesse was right about the jobs.

"If you can help put on a roof, I'll give you one of my horses," a farmer said.

Another job, another roof. Now he had money for the train back to Iowa. Then he heard about the Talbots and was hired immediately.

Ben rented a room in a boarding house and was the best dressed man for miles. Nobody knew he wore Jesse's suits, shirts, and hats. Well, why not? Someone might as well use them.

He shook his head now. If he had followed Jesse to Seattle, he would never have met Emily.

Ben thought back to earlier that day. He had gone out to his acreage, the property he had worked for. The Talbots had changed their mind, building their new home on the opposite slopes of the Willamette, claiming they had a better view on that side. The price for ten acres was reasonable and in no time he had enough to pay for the parcel, plus barter for the team. His partner, John Creel would lay a foundation once weather permitted and care for the horses until he returned.

He stood on the cliff overlooking the Willamette River. It was a clean river. Deep and clear. A dazzling blue-green, the river was fed by the melting winter snows of Mount Hood. Majestic with rivers, lakes and streams, and snow-capped mountains, Oregon boasted an abundance of natural resources. Rain fell often in the fertile valley, so the farmer didn't worry about water for his crops. Unfortunately, the rain also turned the roads into slick mud and mud oozed beneath his boots as he walked across his property.

Rocky bluffs, rose on either side of the river. It was a sight he would never tire of, as Iowa was as flat as a sheet. Ben understood why settlers referred to this land as God's country. It was God's country. Hadn't God led Lewis and Clark over this new territory a century ago? Hadn't people been coming to settle it since that discovery?

And though Ben's skills lay with carpentry, he knew the land would always be a part of him. He wondered now how Emily felt about land. The trees? The river? Somehow he knew that she loved the trees and it was because of that he only cleared off enough land for the house. If necessary, more could be cleared later.

Church. Ben had never been part of a corporate body, but it didn't mean that he did not believe. He believed with all his heart and soul. Too many things had happened in his life not to believe. The wagon accident when the horses got spooked. Thrown clear, he had escaped with a bump on his head. There was the time when he was delirious with the fever and didn't know his own family. Vaguely he recalled cool cloths, mustard compresses, muffled voices as prayers floated over his head. When at last he opened his eyes, his mother said, "Thank You, God, for giving me back my son." There'd been a wintry night when he was caught in a sudden, blinding snowstorm and almost didn't find his way home.

No. God had a Hand in his life. He believed it with all his heart. God had also sent him here to Oregon country. Emily had gone to the dance that night, and it was as if God had brought them together for a reason. He was never more sure of anything.

Ben looked out over his land again. As soon as possible, he wanted to buy more parcels, so he could build. Houses. Buildings. Shops. Whatever was needed. At thirty, it was time to settle down. To marry. Raise a family. Get going on his business. Yes, he had left Iowa behind, and if it hadn't been for Ma and Pearl and his promise to his father, he wouldn't be returning now.

Pearl, strong and solid like their mother, would find a

man in Oregon to marry. Lulu had gone to California three years before, marrying a man in gold country. And Clara, married to a teacher, moved with her husband to his home in Connecticut. Anna, dedicated to nursing, would stay in Iowa. Of course she could find people to care for no matter where she lived. Albert was in Washington State, on some peninsula, fishing the waters of the Pacific, claiming this would be his permanent home. And Jesse. Seattle. Eureka. San Francisco. Who knew where he would be next month, next year.

Ben reached down and picked up a clump of earth. Dark. Solid. Good dirt. He wondered if Emily would care if they didn't farm? Would she be proud to be the wife of a builder? He dropped the dirt and looked into the cloudless winter sky. First he must convince her that he was worthy of her. Convince her that he wasn't a heathen. She hadn't said the word, but her eyes told what her lips did not.

The trip lay heavy on his mind. He wanted to stay to court Emily. All he wanted was a fighting chance. His prayers to God had been clear on that point. Maybe it was time to wait to see what God had in mind. Maybe it was time he learned patience though patience had never been one of his strengths.

He thought of a verse he had memorized years ago. *I waited patiently for the Lord; and he inclined unto me, and heard my cry.* (Psalm 40:1)

He ran a hand through his thick hair. Time for a cut and a mustache trim. Or should he grow a beard? Seemed most men wore beards in Oregon. Not that he needed more hair on his head. Still, beards did look dashing.

He thought again of brother Jesse and the tweed suit. It was the tweed that first caught the eyes of Kate Russell. Happy-go-lucky Kate. He had her to thank for Emily. It was at a dance he told her he had heard the candy factory was hiring. If she hadn't gone to work and met Emily, he would never have seen her and fallen in love.

His heart tightened at the thought of her. The gentle smile. Her high cheekbones. The eyes. Not just the color, though they were a beautiful blue, but the expression. Yes, there were stories in those eyes and he aimed to discover what they were. There was also pain there, and he would find out what caused the pain and maybe help erase it. Even if he couldn't hold her as he wanted to, she helped fill the aching emptiness. And he would forever remember how she had felt as they waltzed around the floor at the grange hall. It had felt good. Right. Surely God understood his intentions.

A breeze flew in from the river and sudden clouds scudded across the sky. Rain was brewing. It was time to go pack.

The train would take three days. Steam engines were a marvel, but Ben wished he could arrive in a day, return in half a day. He couldn't sleep on the trains. They were noisy and soot landed on everything. When he arrived at the farm, he would sleep around the clock, then be ready to sell, to pack, to look forward to his return trip to Oregon. Back to Emily. His mother would love her. He had never doubted it for a minute.

Ben took one last look at the river, turned, and walked down the hill toward the waiting carriage and the new team of horses. Two lumps of sugar waited in his pocket.

ten

The benches had been polished and a coat of paint applied to the basement walls.

"I think it's silly," Beulah scoffed. "It isn't as if it matters one whit."

"Don't thee like to put thy best foot forward?" Grandfather said. "I think it's fine."

"Humph!" That's as far as Beulah ever went when it came to disapproval of something her husband said or did.

Pastor Luke Morrison was arriving on the train the day after tomorrow. Just in time for the new year. A boarding house was located close to the meetinghouse for him to live in temporarily. He would buy a horse and buggy soon after his arrival, and make definite plans then for his living quarters.

Emily tried to get caught up in all the excitement, but her mind kept whirling with thoughts of Ben Galloway. It didn't matter how many times she told herself she was being foolish, she couldn't get the image out of her head and heart. It had only been a few days since she had seen him, but there was an emptiness she had never felt before. A feeling different from when she left her parents so many years ago.

At least she needn't worry about wearing her best dress as she dressed that First Day morning. The gray was the only suitable dress for meeting. She wanted to wear the silver clasp in her hair, but it would remain in her night stand, just as the blue velvet dress stayed in the depths of

Kate's closet. She could well imagine how many eyebrows would be raised if she dared ever wear that to meeting.

She brushed her hair a few extra strokes, and braided it quickly.

"Are thee ready?" Grandmother called from the foot of the stairs.

"Coming." She picked Black Beauty up, then set him back in his hiding place.

"I dare say I bet everyone will be there this morning," Grandmother Beulah said. "I just hope he's a true man of God."

When the meetinghouse came into view, it appeared indeed that every one had come, and had arrived early. Grandfather let Grandmother off, then went to hitch the horses.

They had to sit in the back, except for Emily. She slipped up to the front to play a few opening hymns.

Starting the second song, "Blessed Assurance," she was aware of a sudden quietness, following by hushed whispers. Emily turned to see Pastor Luke Morrison entering by a side door.

Short with a wiry build, his face was covered with a full, dark beard and mustache. He turned just as Emily looked up and their eyes locked on each other. Emily missed a chord. He nodded, indicating with his hand that he wanted her to stop playing. She didn't even finish the stanza, but took her hands from the keys and waited.

"Welcome, welcome, my friends of God." The voice was low and had a resonant sound. "Shall we pray together." It was a statement, not a question. It was a good, solid, commanding voice and Emily wondered what Grandmother was thinking. Ben's voice had more inflection, and Emily's mind couldn't help comparing. Pastor Luke had a stocky, frame, while Ben's was angular and lean.

Luke made her think of a picture she had seen of President James Madison. 'Short of stature, but mighty of mind,' the caption had read. Was Pastor Luke Morrison mighty of mind, also?

Emily took her place on the bench and lowered her head as the silence settled in around her. But try as she might, she could not concentrate on her prayers this morning. Instead, she repeated a few Bible verses and waited.

The prayer time was longer than usual and she wondered if that was Luke's usual custom, or did he want every one to know his heart was open to God's leading, God's command his will?

Trembling, she thought of that First Day with Kate sitting next to her. It had been a wonderful time, following a night of joy, then pain. Now she had to put that night out of her mind once and for all and listen to what this man had to say. Prepare her mind for what might be forthcoming. If Grandmother had any say in the matter, Emily and Pastor Luke would soon be betrothed. Surely he had been picked by God to be the husband of the spinster Emily Drake.

Emily looked up to find Pastor Luke staring at her. How long had he been watching her? She lowered her head, her face turning pink. What was he thinking? Perhaps he was studying the congregation to see how many mouths moved in silent prayer. She folded her hands, wishing suddenly she didn't have to sit so close to the front where he could see her every move.

He cleared his throat.

"Let's sing another hymn. This is a favorite of mine and I hope yours, too. I've been told that our pianist doesn't need music to read from. "Will you please join me in singing, 'Faith of Our Fathers.'"

Emily made her way to the piano, her fingers touching the keys and rippling up and down the keyboard.

"Faith of our fathers! living still. In spite of dungeon, fire, and sword. O how our hearts beat high with joy, When-e'er we hear that glorious word!"

There was a brief message, prayer, and again silent prayer. Emily sat straight, and felt her hand go numb from clutching her handkerchief so tightly.

At last the meeting drew to a close. She rose and was about to hurry down the aisle when Pastor Luke motioned for her to wait.

"The playing was magnificent, Miss Emily." He held out his hand. "Are there any hymns you don't know?"

His gaze was penetrating and Emily tried to relax. "If I've heard it once, I can usually play it, Pastor Morrison."

"That's excellent. Wonderful." His hand touched her shoulder as he began walking. "I must go talk and meet some of the people. I'll see you later since I'll be having the afternoon meal at your home."

Emily nodded, but no words came out of her mouth.

"Oh, Emily, what did you think of Pastor Morrison?" Myrtle Lee chortled, suddenly standing at Emily's side. Her dark eyes were expressive.

She didn't say it, but Emily knew what she was thinking. She half-curtsied. "It's so nice to see you, Mrs. Harper. Do have a good First Day."

Myrtle Lee started to sputter, but Emily pressed on, not wanting to be detained any longer. Anything she might say or do would be noticed, and soon everyone would know what she had said. It was far easier to keep her mouth closed.

Emily was glad that Pastor Luke was coming, though she was always tongue-tied around people she didn't know, and if she did say something, it sounded dumb. Of course Grandmother would take over the conversation so she need not worry about it. A simple "yes" or "no" was all that was required.

Since Pastor Luke did not have a horse or buggy yet, and the Drakes' had limited space, Mr. James offered to bring him over. Later, Grandfather would drive him home as there would be plenty of room for just the two of them.

They arrived home and Emily slipped an apron over her gray muslin. She pushed back a loose strand of hair at the nape of her neck. There wasn't time for pins, or to worry about what she looked like.

Emily had a good feeling about Pastor Luke. She liked his manner. He appeared confident, as his voice resonated through the meeting. Surely God had sent this man to Portland, to the Society of Friends for a reason. Emily believed that everything happened for the best, that God had a plan for her life, and for all who believed in Him. Could Luke (she could think of him in her thoughts as Luke, but never to his face—it would show lack of respect) be the answer to long spoken prayers? Would he be interested in remarrying one day? Should she even think about him in that way? One day she knew she wanted to have a husband and children. Yet, even as the thoughts went through her mind, she had difficultly forgetting another face, a warm smile, and the piercing gaze.

Slices of ham, canned snap beans from last year's garden, boiled small potatoes from the root cellar, and chunks of yesterday's bread was placed on the table. Grandmother's berry compote and blackberry jam rounded out the menu. Slices of Christmas fruit cake and Emily's sponge cake would be served with tea and coffee in the parlor later.

Horses pulled up out front, just as Grandmother poked

another stick of wood in the stove. Sudden clouds had blown across the sky as rain threatened. The knock came. Grandfather went to answer as Emily felt her stomach churn. "Come in, do come in, Pastor Morrison."

Luke's presence seemed to fill the room, his voice booming out, as he shook hands with Grandfather, then nodded at Grandmother in the kitchen. "Afternoon, Mrs. Drake. And Miss Emily." He removed his hat and overcoat. "I do want you to call me by my first name. Luke or Pastor Luke, if it's all the same to you."

"Dinner will be served shortly," Grandmother said in her no-nonsense tone.

"Here. Come sit by the fire while we wait for the women to set the table." Grandfather motioned to a chair by the stove.

The dining room table was set with Grandmother's best linen tablecloth and matching napkins. Four place settings of the good china and sterling silver were placed on the snow white cloth. It seemed strange having a fourth person sitting at the table, as the Drakes rarely had company. Emily used to wonder why, but inviting the preacher was different. It was an expected gesture. Emily fetched the butter from the pantry, and put the compote and jam on.

"Thee can both come to the table," Grandmother called out.

Emily sat across from Luke, who bowed his heard for their silent thanksgiving. When she glanced up, their eyes met. She was the first to look away.

"Oregon is beautiful country, and I 'spect I'll get used to the rain," he was saying. He spoke with a slight accent, a "Midwestern twang" is what Grandfather had called it on the way home from meeting.

"Rain is what makes our crops grow," Grandfather said.

Emily listened to the banter. Words were rarely spoken when there was just the three of them, but Grandfather carried the conversation now and it amused Emily.

She watched out of the corner of her eye, not wanting Luke to catch her looking. She might have entered the conversation—now they were talking about horses—but she would rather listen and let her thoughts take over.

"I'm sure you can get a fine horse if you ask at the livery stable," Grandfather explained. "Ol' Bob will tell you who to see for the best price."

The food wasn't going down at all well. Emily left half a slice of bread on her plate, then smiled at Grandmother when she frowned. She felt a stirring inside, a nervousness, but it wasn't the same as she'd felt toward Ben. Quite the opposite. It was important to look what was inside a person. And she knew what was inside Pastor Luke. A love of God. Pure and simple. Emily also knew she would never feel about Luke or any man as she had that night dancing in Ben's arms. She trembled now at the memory. Yet meeting Luke was ordained.

Pastor Luke scooted his chair back and nodded toward Beulah. "Fine dinner, Mrs. Drake. Thank you for inviting me."

"Let's take our dessert into the parlor," Grandmother said. "I'll bring the teapot."

Emily carried the tray with the dessert plates, forks, and slices of cake.

The heavy drapes, usually drawn, were opened to let a small amount of sunshine in from the window that faced east. The organ sat in one corner and the French Provincial chair, an heirloom from Grandmother's side of the family, sat in a conspicuous spot in the opposite corner.

Nobody ever sat there. Emily much preferred the rocking chairs in the dining area next to the wood stove, over the ornate furnishings of the parlor. She sat on one end of the chesterfield, and watched as Luke chose a rocking chair next to the organ.

Soon they were comfortably settled and Emily watched and listened as she sipped her tea. She couldn't have gotten a word in edgewise if she'd wanted to. *Silly for even worrying about knowing what to say.*

"Rachel, my wife," Pastor Luke began. He looked at the floor, his hand setting the saucer down on the table. "She died six months ago, but it seems like just yesterday at times, and at other times it seems she has been gone forever."

"It must have been tragic for you," Grandmother said. "And thy child?"

"It was a little boy—a breech birth. There was nothing the doctor could do. If we'd lived in the city close to the hospital, she and the child might have been saved, but my meetinghouse was in Fern Hollow, twenty miles from the nearest town. And the doctor was late in coming. Rachel kept saying she'd be all right, that often it takes longer for a first child." His eyes looked tortured and Emily found her heart going out to him. "If only I'd followed my first God-given instinct. I could have wrapped her warmly in the wagon and driven her to town."

"Has thee thought about marrying again one day?"

Luke nodded. "A man needs a woman at his side, especially a preacher. There's the calling on the sick, visitation. I need someone who feels led in that direction." His eyes focused on Emily momentarily, then looked away.

"It's too soon, however," he said, setting his cup down. "I am not over my wife. I feel she is with me. I still love her as if she was."

An awkward silence settled around the four, until Beulah spoke. "Take thy time, Pastor Luke. Thee will know when the time is right, when the right person comes along."

Pastor Luke was again talking about his wife and how she had written his letters, visited the sick, played the piano, and raised a garden, plus keeping the house up and sewing their wardrobe. "One couldn't have had a better mate," he went on.

Emily nibbled on the edges of her cake, then set the fork down. She was afraid Grandmother would begin espousing her virtues, and it would be embarrassing. She didn't look up, not wanting to see Luke's expression, not wanting to decipher what he might be thinking. She sipped the last drop of tea, trying to shake the memory of the night—the one night that would forever haunt her—the night she had gone to the forbidden dance. Would it matter if she never told anyone? She had prayed for forgiveness, so why couldn't she let it go? With Ben gone back to Iowa now, it should be easier. She'd somehow get on with her life.

"Emily would you mind playing a few hymns before we pray?" Pastor Luke asked, motioning toward the organ.

Grandmother nodded. "Certainly."

Emily rose, wishing Grandmother would let her answer for herself just once.

"Our First Days are spent in prayer and reading the Word," Grandfather said. "A quiet time so we can feel God's presence."

"I'm sure God honors music," Pastor Luke said. "There'll be plenty of the afternoon left for silence, Mr. Drake."

Emily played three hymns and Luke's deep bass filled

the room. The sound of his voice sent chills up her spine.

"Now, come sit, Emily. We'll pray before I leave." It was obvious Pastor Morrison was used to having the final say in matters.

They prayed for each member of the Meeting as Beulah Drake explained the various needs of the people.

Pastor Luke read from Second Thessalonians, chapter three. "Pray for us. . .:that the word of the Lord may have free course, and be glorified, even as it is with you, And that we may be delivered from unreasonable and wicked men; for not all men have faith. But the Lord is faithful, who shall stablish you, and keep you from evil."

Emily repeated the words, and her heart plummeted. "For not all men have faith." *Ben.* She did not know about his faith. How deep it went.

The prayers were short, yet meaningful. She knew without looking at Grandmother's face that she was pleased that Pastor Luke knew the Lord, and was filled with righteousness.

"It's time for me to go, and I thank thee for the wonderful dinner and your fine hospitality." He nodded toward Beulah, then Harrison. He paused for a brief moment, his eyes meeting Emily's. It looked as if he wanted to say something, but he extended his hand, clasped Emily's, covering it with his other hand. "I need someone to write a few letters each week. Do you think you could do that for me?"

"Of course," Grandmother began, but Luke held his hand up.

"It's for Miss Emily to decide. If she has the time."

Emily nodded, removing her hand from his firm grasp. His hands were warm, responsive. She had felt a safe comfort, and though his eyes held pain, they were sincere.

From somewhere deep within, she sensed that he was a caring person and Emily was glad he had come to Portland, glad he would be their pastor.

"I would be honored to write letters for thee when I am not working. Seventh Day afternoons would be best."

"Good. It's settled." He looked around the room, then bowed slightly. "I will see thee at meeting tonight?"

"Of course," was Beulah's reply. "Bless thee, Pastor Luke, and do come calling again." The meaning was not lost on the other people in the room.

Emily listened as Grandfather went out to hitch up the horses, picking up the dishes and cups as Grandmother stood on the porch, following Pastor Luke Morrison down the steps. She breathed a sigh of relief. There was nothing to fear of this man. His kind gentleness had reached out, encompassing her. It was as if he was assuring her that yes, indeed, she was worthy, and that he was going to bring about a change in her life. She didn't dare to wonder in which way. . .

Emily's Sponge Cake

Separate 3 large eggs.

Add to yolks—2/3 cup cold water and beat until it
    forms 1 quart of foam.

Beat in gradually—1¼ cups sugar.

Add 1 scant tsp. baking powder to 1½ cups flour,
    which has been sifted 3 times.

Add to sugar and egg yolks.

Add 1½ tsp. cream of tartar and 1 pinch of salt to
    the stiffly beaten egg whites.

Fold into yolk mixture.

Flavor with lemon extract.

Pour into an ungreased angel-food cake pan.

Bake in a very slow oven (350) about 45 minutes.

The cake Emily served to Pastor Luke Morrison the first time
he came to Sunday dinner. It was a family recipe that had
been handed down.

eleven

Sarah Galloway, never a beauty but coming from good, healthy stock, beamed with pride as she thought about her children. She and Pa had been mightily blessed, though he never thought of it that way. Her heart constricted now. Jesse, the oldest, was the only one to break her heart. He was handsome. Worldly. Too self-centered. He hadn't even cried when he'd heard that Pa had died. Where had they gone wrong with Jesse? Only the Lord knew.

Sarah rose and put another log on the fire. Pearl sat by the window, stitching tea towels for her hope chest. She was a good girl. Dutiful. Quiet. Loving. A real blessing to Sarah in her old age. Pearl managed the chores Sarah found too difficult, and had even plowed and planted corn last spring. She had her mother's raw-boned build, her strong constitution. She could do the work of any man and seemed to take pleasure in doing so since she was now in charge of the house.

Closing her eyes, she thought of Benjamin. She never knew why, but she had favored him from the time he was pressed into her waiting arms. The second child, second son, there was something about those eyes that seemed to focus at such a young age, the brightness obvious to others. Jesse, never a loving child, wanted to be left alone, but Benjamin liked to be cuddled. And Sarah had cuddled. And mothered. And loved with all her heart. Now she was troubled. Benjamin still hadn't married, and had chosen to go running off with Jesse to Oregon. Supposedly they would find work there. Was her Benjamin to turn out like his shiftless brother? She prayed not. Yet, why had he left her and Pearl alone to tend to the chores, to eke a living off the land? That wasn't her Benjamin, at least not the Benjamin she knew.

She recalled the morning he left. He had hurried back, giving her a kiss and hug. "Sure you don't want to come, Ma?"

"I cain't," was her reply. "I have to stay here. Be close to Pa."

Pa, buried in the small graveyard two miles down the road, had been Sarah's love, her lifeline. The only problem between the couple had been his lack of faith. She had lived her beliefs, hoping Jebediah would come to believe in the Master, to know there was a power stronger than he.

"Don't take to believing in something I can't see," had been his answer. "It's okay for you and I'll go along with your larning the kids this 'religion' bit, but just don't expect me to believe, too."

A slim, yet strong man, Jeb had earned money as a craftsman. He built sturdy tables, chairs, and shelves. People came from miles to buy his beautiful creations. And though Sarah had prayed that Benjamin would take after her and prefer farming the land, from an early age he showed a keen interest in wood. His dreams were loftier than his Pa's. He had shared them with Sarah, telling her he would one day build her a house.

"I'm not a farmer, Ma. I knew that the first time we planted corn." His dark eyes shined as he talked about his dreams. Like father, like son, yet Ben was different. So different.

Sarah felt sudden tears blinding her vision. Jeb had been a good man. A loving husband. A strict, yet caring father.

And Sarah had never given up, never stopped saying prayers, asking God for living proof of His existence so she could show Jeb. Sarah had thought of Thomas and how he, too, had not believed, yet saw Jesus after the Resurrection, had put his fingers in Jesus' side and came to believe.

Jeb didn't have that opportunity, and as far as Sarah knew, had gone to his grave an unbeliever.

"I'm going to make some gingerbread," Sarah said, now, breaking the silence.

Pearl set her embroidery aside. "Ma, you feel all right?"

"Course I do." She turned and smiled at her youngest. At fourteen, Pearl's face was too long, her expression sallow. She missed her Pa and her brothers. Like Sarah, she knew Pearl missed Benjamin the most. And Anna. Of all of them, Anna would be the most likely one to come home for a visit. It was this sudden prompting that told her they needed something to go with coffee.

Christmas had come and gone and though they read the Christmas story in Luke and sang a few Christmas carols, the day had passed by like any other. Sarah had knit Pearl a hat and matching mittens, and Pearl's gift to her had been a pair of warm, woolen socks.

"No use sittin' if I can do something, now is there? Besides you like gingerbread, and the fire's still hot from supper."

"No use in thinkin' that Benjamin's coming," Pearl said in a wistful voice. "We ain't heard a thing in two months. He's done found himself a job and probably a wife."

Sarah shook her gray head, her hands smoothing the apron over her calico skirt. "Benjamin doesn't have a wife yet. He's a looking, I know, but he's fussy and most women aren't to his liking."

"He's found one in Oregon, Ma. Mark my words. He probably won't come back, though he promised."

"Ben's coming home, child. I know him. He wouldn't say so, if he didn't intend to keep his promise."

Pearl said nothing as she picked up the embroidery again.

The fire was stoked, the gingerbread baking. Later Sarah would cover it with a cloth, and sit it on the sideboard for morning.

Sarah left the bowl and spoons in the sink. She would wash them in the morning's light, conserving the kerosene. Pearl had already gone to bed, leaving Sarah alone with her thoughts.

She sat in the darkness of the house, the only home she and Jeb had ever had. She knew every nook and cranny. Loved every plank from top to bottom. She'd helped build this place. Six months before the birth of Jesse, she'd pounded nails and helped her husband proudly. Let the others roam all over the continent, but she was content to stay in Iowa. On her land, close to Jeb and the cemetery.

She thought about latching the front door, but they were safe in these parts. Never had anybody bother them; no reason to think things had changed. Sarah looked out the window, noticing how brilliant the stars shone from the black sky. It was late. Much later than she usually stayed up, but for some reason she felt a restlessness.

Tucking the quilt around Pearl's lean body, she slowly walked to her bed, the bed she'd shared with Jeb. Kneeling on the braided rug, she offered first her thanks for her many blessings, then prayers for her children, asking protection for each one.

"And, if You don't mind, dear God, please remember Jebediah. He was a good man, even if he never did come to believe."

It was in the middle of the night sometime. Sarah had been dreaming. In her dream, Jeb was holding her hand as Anna stood over her, smiling. Off to the right were her children, all but Benjamin. Then through the hazy midst, Benjamin strolled in, his face shining, his thick, bushy hair sticking straight out as it always had.

"Ma, I found me someone. I just had to come tell you about her. Her name is Emily."

Sarah shook her head, but the voice was there, and a large, callused hand held hers. She opened her eyes and gasped. "Benjamin! It is you, or am I sick with the fever?"

"No, Ma. It's me. I got home an hour ago, but decided to let you rest."

Sarah gathered the quilts around her as she sat up. "I had the most wonderful dream. We were all together, even Pa. But I remember something about an *Emily*."

Benjamin hugged his mother, then stepped back. "That part wasn't a dream, Ma. It was for real. I'll go out so you can get dressed, then we need to talk."

An hour later, the cow was milked, side meat was frying, and biscuits were baking in the old wood stove. Ben decided to wait to tell his mother about Emily, his land, and the move.

"Ma, you know how to make a place smell homey."

"I should." She smiled, then reached over and hugged him again. "Been doin' this a good long time."

Pearl came in, stomping her feet. "Where'd you get the horse, Ben? He's beautiful."

"A man in town. He's on loan. That and the wagon."

"What do you need another wagon for?" Ma asked.

Ben took a deep breath. He knew this wasn't going to be easy. He realized how Ma felt about the farm. How she wouldn't want to leave Pa. He'd have to do some tall talking. It would wait until breakfast was over, unless she pressed him.

After a second cup of coffee and a third slice of ginger-bread, Ben found his thoughts on Emily again. Not that she ever strayed far from his mind. He wondered if she could cook like Ma. Somehow, he didn't doubt for a moment that she knew about cooking, planting a garden, and keeping house. That, plus dipping chocolates. He remembered the small package he'd brought for Ma and Pearl. He figured neither Ma or Pearl had ever had a chocolate covered bonbon.

"Brought you something special," he said then. "A real treat."

"Just coming home, seeing your face is all I need," Sarah said, drinking in the sight of her favorite son.

"If you don't want them, Pearl will," he said winking at his baby sister.

Ma's eyes widened when she lifted the lid. "Candy. I never seen anything this pretty before. Where on earth—"

"A friend made them, Ma. A very good friend."

Pearl paused, a chocolate half way to her mouth. "Didn't I tell you, Ma?"

He hadn't planned on sharing Emily with them just yet, but now he had to.

"You already mentioned this Emily," Sarah said.

Ben nodded. "That's right, I did. And Ma, you'll love her. She's everything I've ever dreamed about. Tiny. A lot shorter than Pearl. And has the prettiest eyes you've ever seen. She belongs to the Friends' Church, Ma. She doesn't believe in dancing and rings and make-up."

"You going to give up dancing?"

"Yes, Ma. I can do that."

Pearl touched her brother's arm. "Does Emily love you,

Benjamin?"

"I. . .don't know for certain, but if her eyes are any indication, she cares for me." He remembered how she'd felt in his arms waltzing across the floor, the way her cheek had felt against his lips, but he didn't talk about that.

"There are women here who would marry you, give you children," Sarah broke in. "I can list them on my fingers."

"Ma, I know, I know. But it's Emily that I love. I've never been more sure of anything in my life."

"Do you have a place, Benjamin?"

"Yes, Ma, I do. Ten acres. You'll never believe how rich the earth is. You can have your garden, and Pearl can help out, or go to school. There's a school nearby. It wouldn't be a far walk, or maybe she can take one of the horses." He knew that one of Ma's wishes were for her children to be schooled since she hadn't gone but a few years. Her father hadn't believed in education for "wimmin" as he called them. Benjamin had gone through eighth, two grades further than Pa had.

"Please don't ask me to leave Pa," Sarah said, getting up to pour more coffee. "I can't do it, son."

"Ma, you're not leaving him. He'd want you to go. He'd want you to be with me, you know he would."

Pearl sat beside the window, looking out, her hands in her lap. Ben wondered why she wasn't helping him convince their mother—why she hadn't said a word on either one's behalf.

"Baby sister, what are you thinking?" Ben asked then, hoping for an ally.

"I'm with Ma, Ben. I can always come to Oregon later." She didn't speak of death, but both knew Sarah wouldn't live forever.

"Ma, I have to go back. I promised Emily."

His mother's mouth pressed together tightly. She was a loving woman, but could also be stubborn. "I only hope you know what you're doing. Having your heart set on someone who, for all you know, may be married by the time you get back to Ory-gone."

Ben knew it to be true, but he had to return. He had asked her to wait and he had to believe that she would.

"Seems you promised you'd come back here."

"And I came, didn't I?"

"But, not to stay—"

Ben shook his head. "Not when I've found a place more beautiful than you can imagine."

"I'm not going to see Pa again," Sarah said. I need to be here with him so we can talk over things."

"Ma, life is for the living."

Sarah fidgeted with her apron and looked out the window to the meadow stretching as far as one could see. It was cleared and straight and even as God had made it. How could she leave the land she'd harvested? How could she leave Jeb and his grave? The home they'd built together? Yet how could she stay here and keep Pearl from attending school?

"I'll go to Ory-gone with you," she said finally, "but I must pay your father one final visit."

"I'll come, too," Ben said.

Ben realized that they had never talked about that day. The words had stayed locked up in his heart until now.

As they trudged up the tiny knoll where Sarah had insisted Jeb be buried, Ben's voice filled the crisp morning air. "He's with the Lord, you know, Ma."

She didn't turn, but placed a tiny bouquet of dried flowers on the barren grave. "Oh, I wish it were so, Benjamin, but I know he never came to believe."

"Yes, he did, Ma."

"No, son, you're wrong."

"Ma, remember when I was with him that last night?"

Sarah recalled Benjamin sitting beside him, recalled the talk about the first little bear Benjamin had whittled from a piece of soft pine. Pa had actually laughed. She'd left to fix supper so didn't hear anymore, but Ben stayed with his father, helping him drink, saying he would eat later.

"That night, Ma, when you slept in the rocker, Pa asked me to pray with him. I told you—"

"You never told me a thing about praying with Pa."

"He asked me about salvation, and I told him he had to ask for forgiveness, and to ask Jesus to come into his heart." Ben couldn't believe he hadn't told Ma. Maybe he had forgotten. He'd fallen, exhausted into bed, asking Pearl to sit with Pa so their mother could sleep. Ma's anguished cry wakened him at day break.

At last it was over and there had been plans to make. A plot to find, a grave to dig. The box Ben had made needed lining. People brought food and blessings. Then prayers were said over the fresh mound of dirt.

It was coming back now. The one time he had tried to talk about it, Sarah had hushed him into silence. Hushed him because she had been aching for her dead husband's soul. Aching for a reason that did not exist. If only Ben had realized.

Ben pulled Sarah up from her knees, and they clung to each other as Sarah sobbed, "Praise You, Father. Oh, thank You so much for answering my prayers."

She turned once more to look back at the grave. "I'm leaving, Pa, there's no reason to stay now. We're off to Ory-gone and a new life. I'll see you in heaven."

If it had been up to Ben, he would have left for Oregon

the next week, but Ma said certain things couldn't be rushed. The farmhouse, land, and most of the furnishings were put up for sale, but many of the items like Ma's bed, the table and chairs, a bookcase, and Pearl's hope chest— all things Pa had made—would be shipped on the freight train. Anna was summoned and would be home soon, to say good-bye before they moved so far away.

While waiting for the house and land to sell, Ben's thoughts were constantly on Emily. She was the force that pushed him on, made him impatient for things to happen so they could leave. Evenings he whittled another horse, then another. One night he sat beside the kerosene lamp, searching for words to write, hoping she would heed them and continue to wait. The letter would be mailed to Kate's house.

> *My Dear Friend, Emily,*
> *It seems like many weeks have passed since I last saw you. There are certain things one cannot write in a letter. There are certain things one must say and do face to face.*
> *I want you to know that I plan to come calling just as soon as I return to Oregon.*
> *My words were truthful that night. I can see you now, eyes glistening as you held the horse in your hand. I am glad you liked my gift.*
> *I beg you, I implore you to wait for my return. My intentions are strictly honorable.*
> >*As ever,*
> >*Benjamin Galloway*

He didn't expect her to answer, but at least she would know he was thinking of her.

People came to look, but Ben held out for a better price.

He needed money to get started on his business in Oregon.

When no more offers came by March, Ben went to town to purchase the train tickets. He'd settle for less, for he sensed he had to leave now.

As Ben walked past the station, his eye caught a "BOOKS" sign in the window of a shop. A book. The perfect gift for Emily. Though he had whittled more horses, he wanted to give her a book. He entered the small shop.

"I'm interested in that book in the window."

The shopkeeper handed it to him. Ben opened the volume, *Leaves of Grass* by Walt Whitman. When he read that Whitman came from a Quaker background, he knew it was perfect. He could see Emily's shy smile now, hear her protest that she couldn't possibly accept it. He plunked down the coins and left the shop whistling.

Putting the book into his pocket, next to the train tickets, Ben stopped at the post office to check for mail. Not that he expected anything, but he had given Kate Ma's address, and had invited her to write. What he really hoped for was a missive from Emily, or at least some word about her.

The postmaster handed him a pink envelope. Kate. It had to be. Who else would write on pink stationery?

One thin sheet fell out.

Ben,
  There isn't much time to write, but I wanted you to know that things have changed since you left. If I were you, I'd hurry back to Oregon. I'm not at liberty to say anything more.
                              Best regards,
                              Katherine Russell

Ben read the letter twice, then jammed it back into the

envelope. His heart sunk. Emily. The "changes" had to do with Emily. And the preacher. What else could Kate have meant? Sudden longing and fear spread through him. He had to get back to Oregon. Could he wait until next week? If he could have found a faster mode of travel, he would have done so. There had been a flight in 1903 out of Kitty Hawk, North Carolina. The Wright Brothers had invented a plane. It had been in all the papers, but as far as Ben knew there were no planes for passengers yet.

Clutching the letter, he closed his eyes and saw those beautiful, violet-blue eyes that had haunted him from the very first moment. His heart ached for Emily's smile, the smile she now bestowed on another man. He saw Oregon. His land. His dream. Emily. She was so much a part of it. God had been so good to him and he must keep believing that Emily would realize that she belonged to him. He must hurry back to court her, to claim her, and to eventually wed her. There was precious little time to waste.

twelve

Emily began working for Pastor Luke the following Saturday. He had located a small house close to the church, and had hired Alfreida, a cleaning lady to come the four hours that Emily would be there. "Just so people won't talk," was his explanation.

She had gone to work not knowing what to expect. Would she do the work he requested satisfactorily? He'd mentioned writing letters. She felt confident in that area. She knew her grammar and spelling were accurate; she'd received A's while in school. She soon learned she had nothing to dread as Luke was quite complimentary about her work.

"You have beautiful handwriting, Emily. Spencerian, isn't it?"

Emily felt embarrassed as she always did when someone admired a quality about her, but remembered what Kate had told her the night of the dance. "Yes, it is," she finally said. "And thank you. I copied the style from a letter my father wrote me once."

"My penmanship is horrific" Pastor Luke replied. "I remember practicing those circles and loops, but the teacher cracked my knuckles because my loops weren't wide enough."

Emily tried to stifle a grin.

"I like it when you smile," he said. "It's better than the frown you usually wear."

"I frown a lot?" she asked. Nobody had ever told her

that before, not even Kate.

"Yes, even when you play the piano. I figure you must have much on your mind."

She felt at ease and was able to relax after the first hour. Half way through the letters, he'd called Alfrieida to bring in a pot of tea and something to eat.

"I want to pay you a fair wage," Pastor Luke said as they munched on cookies.

"But I couldn't accept. It wouldn't be right."

"I insist. I know you must have something you wish for. All women do." He leaned forward. "I only regret I did not realize this before my wife died in my arms. She always wanted to take a trip to New Orleans, ride on a river boat."

Emily stared, sudden compassion filling her. How difficult to know his wife was dying, to be holding her when she drew her last breath. Then to lose the baby two days later.

"I'm so sorry about your wife and son. I know how keenly you must feel your loss."

His fingers tugged at the end of his beard. "Tell me about yourself, Emily. I want to know what is going on inside that head of yours."

"I...can't say for sure," she stammered. How could she tell him that her heart was riddled with memories of a night at a forbidden dance? How could she say she couldn't get a certain face out of her mind? She couldn't tell him that, but she did tell him about her family in California and how her desire was to some day see everyone again.

"That's where your heart is and that is where the wage will go." He sprang to his feet. "I think it is high time you paid your family a visit. The grandparents may not understand, but it's an important consideration for you."

Emily's heart soared. Could it be possible? Like Kate

said, she could and should go one day soon. Perhaps this was an answer to prayer.

❧

January passed, then February. The first week of March had given way to winds and heavy rains. Luke now insisted on taking Emily home after her four hours were completed.

"It gives me a chance to see the countryside and your grandmother always invites me to stay for supper."

Lawns were turning green and the crocuses had peeped their heads up out of the ground still hard from winter's touch. They talked of many things as they rode toward the farmhouse. Luke never had a choice about becoming a minister since he was the oldest son and his father and grandfather before him had all answered the calling.

"Times are changing," he said one Saturday. "Especially here in the West. Having a preacher at the meetings. Lapsing from the old way of talking. Playing music during the service. All good changes, I might add." Luke paused, as if waiting for Emily's comment.

"I like the changes, too," she said. "And I feel you have a calling, Pastor Luke. I see how people respond to you the few times we've visited the sick."

"And you have it also."

They had arrived at Emily's home and the glow from the lamps warmed her heart as she lighted from the buggy.

The one thing Emily had kept buried in her heart was Ben. Not once had she mentioned the dance. She didn't know what Pastor Luke would say, but she had a good idea. Not once did she mention how her heart ached with emptiness when she thought of him. Nor did she mention the thoughts buried deep inside her, or her words, *I will wait.* She tried to forget, to push them aside, but repression did not work. Did Ben still think of her, or had he found someone else more to his liking, someone who danced and could carry on an intelligent conversation?

"Does thee want to talk about it?" Pastor Luke said before they entered the house.

"Talk about what?"

"What it is that makes you suddenly hide from the world. It's as if you go into yourself. That's one of my functions, Emily, to listen to people's problems, hear their prayers."

But she could not tell him about Ben. At least not yet. Though she felt she could discuss most any subject with Luke, she still didn't know what he'd say about her transgression, about her attending a dance. She somehow couldn't face seeing a look of shock, or worse, one of disdain.

Soon they were inside, wraps removed as Emily tended to her usual Seventh Day evening chores.

"Thee is late," Beulah said, stirring a pot on the stove.

"Yes. I'm sorry."

"Does thee know something I do not?"

Emily shook her head. What could her grandmother be thinking? Had she guessed about the wage Luke paid her each week? Could she possibly know that Emily was saving for a trip to California?

"I wrote many letters today," she finally said.

Grandmother might have pressed it further, if Grandfather hadn't called from the dining room, "We need another log for the fire, Emily."

Pastor Luke offered to fetch it, but both grandparents said Emily was used to that chore and he was a guest and shouldn't think about doing such things.

The meal was more quiet than usual, and Emily could feel Luke's eyes on her. She didn't know what he wanted or expected, but sensed something was different, but wasn't sure what.

❧

Work went on as usual at the candy factory and Emily

talked of Luke. Kate listened, but said little. A concerned look crossed her face one morning, but she wouldn't say what was troubling her. Emily had that to puzzle over now.

Emily also worried about Pastor Luke. He would be in the middle of a sentence, then stop, staring into space. She knew he had a wounded heart, because she had seen a hint of tears in his eyes on more than one occasion. When he caught her looking, he lurched to his feet and left the room momentarily.

"Is something wrong?" Emily asked when he returned.

He turned and stared at her in a way that seemed unlike his usual nature. "Emily, I have been pondering about something for a very long while now, almost since that first day I arrived in Oregon."

"Is this something you need to discuss with me?"

"Yes. It concerns you." He walked over and stood in front of her and her mind recaptured the memory of that night when another pair of feet had stopped in front of her, and she'd been forced to look up into the deep brown eyes of Ben Galloway. She'd also been forced to answer his question.

"I need to speak to your grandfather."

Emily stared. What could he be talking about?

"I would like permission to call on you."

She gasped. So this was what the changes were about. The reason he had taken her home the previous weeks. Why hadn't she guessed?

"I see this surprises you."

She lowered her head, not quite knowing what to say.

"I thought you knew that I need a wife to help with my ministry."

Luke was kind. Generous. He loved and served God with all his heart and soul. He was many of the things a woman would want in a man. Why wasn't there a stirring inside her at the thought of his coming to call? She had known all along that everyone thought this was the person God had sent, that it was ordained that they might one day marry, that Luke was the answer to many prayers said on her behalf.

"Everyone thought I would marry you. I won't pretend I didn't hear the talk."

"You said you were still in love with your wife."

"I know." He strode over to the window, and stood with his hands folded behind him. "I do still love Rachel, 'tis true, but life goes on and I need a helpmate. Do thee understand what I am saying?"

Emily nodded, but she wondered why she suddenly felt so awkward, as if she didn't know what to say.

"I'll take thee home now," he said, pushing a book aside. "Forget I said anything. Proper etiquette says I should speak to thy grandfather first."

She was numb as she put on her wraps and went out the door and waited until he helped her into the buggy. Always before they would be chatting, and she'd felt comfortable. Secure. With Luke's declaration, Emily felt sudden apprehension. And then she realized why. Over the past weeks, she'd come to think of him as a brother, the brother she'd left behind in California.

"Are you staying for supper?" she asked.

"I reckon Beulah would think it strange if I did not." His eyes were on her face, but she didn't look at him.

"Emily, I don't want this to change things. I want you to talk to me. I like the way your eyes light up when you tell about something Kate said at work, or how you remembered your father playing the violin. I don't want to lose that special part about you—"

She felt her heart constrict. It was this about Luke that she so admired. He seemed to know what people knew and thought. If only she could tell him about Ben, yet how could she when she couldn't explain it to herself?

Luke let the reins drop for a moment. "I assumed thee knew how I felt."

She had not. Because she felt so comfortable with him, she had let her defenses fall. She had become a person who could talk, who chatted about her family, the needs of the Meeting, the desires of her heart. How could she now tell him she thought of him as a brother? Or explain about Ben? What would he think? She wasn't ready for condemnation.

Luke stayed for supper, but left early. He hardly spoke two words to Emily, and he had not asked Grandfather about the courting. She would have known. Out of deference to her, he had waited. Another thing to admire about him.

After Luke left, the scriptures were read and Emily stayed for prayers, but she could hardly wait to be excused to go to bed. Usually the last to go up, she was the first tonight. With trembling fingers, she began writing in her diary:

> *Mama,*
> *Everything is happening so fast it's hard to be-*
> *lieve. I might be coming on the train to visit you*
> *and Papa. I hope you will write, sending me direc-*
> *tions of how to reach you. I am so eager to come.*
> *Our new pastor is helping me with the expenses in*
> *return for my writing his letters and helping him in*
> *other ways.*

Later she wondered why she didn't mention Luke's declaration that he wanted to come calling. Somehow it stayed inside her where she hoped it would stay. At least for the time being.

thirteen

Ben Galloway had been gone nearly three months. Often it seemed like a dream, but Black Beauty reminded her of his existence and she found the more she tried to get him out of her mind and heart, the more he was there. She prayed at length for deliverance of that night and all that had happened, but it seemed to linger and Emily wondered if she'd ever be free of the memory.

She had thought he might return by now, had hoped to at least hear something through Kate. If Kate heard, she said nothing. Emily continued to work for Pastor Luke, though there was a stiffness between them now. She could feel his eyes on her, watching, waiting, wondering. She had never spoken of Ben and couldn't possibly do so now. If he asked her grandfather about calling on her, he might learn of Ben, but she doubted that the matter would be discussed.

And then he brought it up one afternoon.

"God is much more concerned that we be equally yoked than that we be in love," Luke said.

Love. Was it merely a state of mind? Only a dream, a fairy tale? Perhaps so. Had she only imagined that excitement toward Ben? Was she not to expect it to happen again?

"Have you heard of arranged marriages?" he asked.

"Yes," she said. Was that was this was about? Luke didn't love her after all, but needed someone to help him and this was the answer.

"Originally, I thought that's what we would have. It would be convenient for both of us." He paused, as if

118

waiting for Emily to reply. "But after getting to know you, I realized I care for you very much. Perhaps not as I felt about Rachel, but a quieter type of feeling. You're all the things I could need or ever want. We would take the vows before God and others, and have the blessings from the Meeting."

"I think I understand," Emily finally said.

She did understand, but was it right to marry someone when your heart was with another?

"It's good that we can talk about this. Yes, Rachel is part of me, a part that doesn't want to let go, but I realize I need to get on with my calling. I find you proficient in so many areas. You know the Bible, play the piano, write wonderful letters, and you are a sincere person." He paused momentarily. "I have prayed for clearness and for God's continued guidance and help."

She tried to smile as she lifted her face. How many times had she asked for God's help? How many times had she thought she was over Ben, only to have him haunting her thoughts at work, at night when she wrote in her diary, on a cloudless winter day while she pumped water, or in the pouring rain while she lifted her face for the refreshing wetness that drenched her within minutes.

"If there is no fierce objection, I will speak to your grandfather." He paused, as if waiting for her reply.

She said nothing as he brought her wraps and helped her into her coat.

"I have waited, Emily, as you know." She could feel his eyes on her, watching. "I want you to talk to me."

But she couldn't. The words stayed locked inside her. It seemed she was caught in a whirlpool and no matter what she did, there was no escaping. Would she grow to have a deeper feeling for Luke? Would he some day love her in return, or would Rachel and Ben always be there, reminding them of a previous love?

Emily tried to smile. Luke was good and thoughtful. He had many kind attributes. Why couldn't she feel excitement? Why didn't her heart pound as it had when Ben looked her way? Or was it as Luke said, love wasn't that important?

Luke turned and touched her gloved hand. "I will continue to be in prayer about this, Emily. I only want what God wants for me. For us. I will wait a few more days before speaking to your grandfather."

Luke didn't stay for supper, explaining he had to visit someone who was ill. Emily didn't know if it was true, but was glad that they would be alone.

Later that night, as she always did when she needed solace, Emily turned to her diary. She uncapped the ink and wrote in her thin, spidery handwriting:

Mama,

I wish I knew what your courtship was like, if you loved my father, or if you married because you wanted babies. Was love important then? Did you love my father in the beginning, or did you grow to love him? What if I marry Luke and he doesn't grow to love me? What if he never gets over Rachel? What if I keep thinking about Ben? Those are important things to me. I want marriage. My own home. To have my own baby to love, to dress, to nurse, to just have. I don't think this is wrong for me to feel this way. And I really think God understands my feelings, my heart's desire in this matter. I miss you, Mama. I just wish we could talk about these kinds of things. I need you so bad sometimes. . .

After closing the diary and sinking back under the heavy quilts, Emily knew she had reached a decision. She would say "yes" to Luke's proposal. He needed someone, and so did she. Ben wasn't returning. If so, he would have been back by now. After making her mind up, she was able to sleep, but not before she took Black Beauty and pushed him in the deep recesses of the dresser drawer.

❧

On Monday Kate came to work beaming.

"It came on Friday! My sewing machine! It's so beautiful, Emily, you must come to see it."

"Can I use it?" Emily asked.

Kate hugged her. "Of course. We'll both use it. That was my intention all along."

Kate came the next day with a bolt of the palest pink lawn. "Here. For you, Emily. Enough to make a dress."

Emily's cheeks reddened as she touched the fabric. It was finer than anything she could ever wear. The color was wrong, yet what she wouldn't give to have a dress like this.

"I can't accept this," Emily finally said. "It's beautiful, but I could never pay for it."

"It's a gift," Kate broke in. "A gift from me to you."

"But you shouldn't have bought—"

"I didn't buy it. It was given to me, and I cannot stand this shade of pink. It does nothing for my complexion."

Emily was tempted, but to take such a gift wouldn't be appropriate. "Give the material to someone else."

"I don't want to give it to someone else. It's yours."

Emily held it up to her cheek and wondered what it would look like made into a dress. She put it down. To even think such thoughts was wrong. God knew her thoughts, the desires of her heart, and He expected her to do the right thing.

Kate put the pink lawn back into a bag and smiled. "I'll take it home and start cutting it out tonight. The pattern has tucks in the bodice, and we'll put lace at the neckline."

"I can't accept it—"

"Nonsense," Kate broke in. "You'll accept it because I have no one else to give it to."

Emily turned back to her rows of undipped chocolates. Where would she wear such a dress? Certainly not to meeting, not when everyone would soon know that Luke was courting her.

She glanced at her friend, wanting more than anything to tell her about Luke, but knew it wouldn't be proper, not before he spoke to her grandfather.

As if reading her thoughts, Kate brought up Ben. "He should be home in a few weeks. It'll sure be good to see him again." She paused, looking over at Emily, waiting for her to say something.

"Did you hear from him?"

"No, but I didn't expect to."

Emily's cheeks felt flush.

"What is it?" Kate asked, not one to let anything slip by her.

Emily looked away. "It's nothing."

Kate smiled and touched her friend's arm. "Yes, it is. Now what's going on? If you can't tell your best friend, who can you tell?"

Emily dared not look at Kate.

Kate sighed. "You're not thinking about that preacher fellow, are you?"

"I still work for him."

"I'm not talking about that." Kate's frowned. "When you get all quiet, I know it's something serious. Please tell me that what I'm thinking is not true."

"Meaning?"

Kate stopped working. "Emily, I saw how you looked at Ben, just as I saw how he looked at you. He may not be of your faith, but you love him."

Love. Had it been love? Could it be love? Or was it vastly overrated? How could she dare to hope that love was important? Even if they did love each other, it could go no further. Yet, ever since Luke's words on Saturday, she had visualized Ben, not Luke, in a small cabin on the land she had heard about. She would cook his evening meal in the wood stove when he arrived home as his heavy boots stomped off the mud before entering their home. He would always be happy to see her, taking her into his arms, cuddling her head to his thick chest. There would be a kiss before supper, a hug, and lots more of that after the evening sun went down. They would share a life, a bed, love for God and their fellowman, and bright hopes for the future. And a baby. There would be a baby that looked just like Ben with that impossible, thick, unruly hair. And maybe his bushy eyebrows, and ears that stuck out. And children, both looking just like him.

"You're smiling, Emily Drake and you haven't told me what's amusing. It isn't fair! I demand to know what's going in that head of yours." Kate's red earrings bobbed in the light, her eyes twinkling from teasing.

Emily was brought back to the presence, back to the chocolates and her friend's voice, her growing exasperation. "Pastor Luke is a nice, gentle man."

"And so are most fathers, but you don't marry them," Kate said. "Kindness and gentleness do not make up for love."

"I never said I loved Ben."

"You didn't have to. Come on, let's have our dinner."

The two women left their work station, heading for the small room where they ate each day. They were alone so Emily could talk freely.

"Luke needs a wife. I need a husband."

Kate shook her head. "You're talking about an arranged marriage?"

"Yes, something like that."

"You can't do it, Emily." She handed her a celery chunk. "You'd be miserable."

"How do you know that?"

"Because you love Ben. How many times do I need to say it?"

"We've never spoken of such things."

"No, but he would have before he left. He would have seen you every day if you'd have allowed it. He wanted to speak to your grandfather about calling on you."

"You don't know that, Kate."

"Yes, I do."

"You never said anything to me."

"What good would it have done? What good is it doing now?"

Emily felt tears threaten. Kate was partly right, because Ben had asked her to wait for his return. If that was speaking his mind, then, yes, he had spoken it.

"Luke is a good choice because he loves God and has chosen to serve God and His people."

"What makes you think Ben doesn't love God?"

"He doesn't serve Him."

"No, but that shouldn't make a difference. Not all men can serve God as a preacher. There are leaders and there are followers. Most of us are followers. In fact," Kate went on, "I happen to know that Ben is a leader. He is going to start his own construction company once he gets back. He told me about it. He's already drawn plans for the house he will build on the Oregon City property. If you had shown the slightest interest, he would have taken you there."

"There wasn't time."

Kate folded her napkin, tucking it into her coat pocket. "You're right. There wasn't."

"Anyway, I've all but decided to marry someone of my faith. Besides," she hesitated, "love isn't as important as people make it out to be. One can grow into love. It happens all the time."

"Yes, perhaps it does. But, you my dear girl, have not taken one thing into consideration."

"Which is—?"

"It doesn't work well when one person is already in love with someone else."

She thought about that the rest of the afternoon. Kate was right. What might happen if she married Luke? Could she forget Ben once and for all, or would the memory of that night slip into her thoughts? It took time. She had to give herself time.

Emily filled a red box with the needed rows of chocolates, and closed the lid. There'd been a large order from a company in California and both women were working on it.

"Emily, if you don't love this man, and you take those vows to love, honor, cherish, and obey, it's like a promise and we talked about promises before."

Kate was silent the rest of the afternoon and Emily's heart was heavy. She missed her friend's banter, the laughter. Kate always put her in a good mood. Would they stop being good friends?

When five-thirty came, Kate hurried out of the work area,

grabbed her coat, and shot out the door before Emily had her apron off.

Emily watched Kate walk in the opposite direction toward the streetcar. She had made her angry, but she didn't understand why. It wasn't wrong to marry Luke. As he said, an arranged marriage benefited both, especially when there was a mutual need.

When Emily turned into the lane to the house, she saw Luke's horse and buggy. Sudden apprehension filled her. He hadn't said anything last night at prayer meeting about stopping by. Had he come to speak to her grandfather?

Grandmother was in the kitchen slicing potatoes when Emily walked in. "Thee took longer than usual."

"We had to fill a large order."

"Pastor Luke is in the parlor with your grandfather."

Emily removed her coat and hat. Suddenly she felt shy again. How should she look at him now? It was all different and her first inclination was to turn and run back outside.

Grandmother dried her hands on her apron. "Luke has asked if he might start calling on thee."

So, it was true. Trembling, she started setting four plates out.

"Thee certainly is quiet about this," Grandmother said, pausing to cast a sideways glance in Emily's direction.

"Yes," Emily finally answered.

"Thee knew about it already?"

Emily nodded as she filled the glasses with water.

"Well, aren't thee happy? Thee has been thinking about Pastor Luke, hasn't thee?"

"I don't love him, grandmother, nor he me."

"I didn't love thy grandfather, either."

Somehow Emily knew that was what her Grandmother

would say. She wondered, again, what it had been like for Mama. Had there been love between her parents? Grandmother might know.

"Did my mother and father love each other?"

"I can certainly say for thy father, but not thy mother."

"And?"

"Thy father needed a wife. Thy mother was pretty. She was also strong and well-built."

"Well-built?" What did Grandmother mean? And why did that matter?

"Men often look at how a woman is built. If she looks as if she could bear children, they ask for her hand in marriage."

"You mean he didn't love her?"

"I rather doubt it, Emily."

Emily found it hard to assimilate. A woman was sought after because she had good bones, sort of like a man buying a cow because she looked strong and healthy.

"Apparently Pastor Luke didn't look for that criteria when he married the first time."

Grandmother nodded. "Yes, thee is right, I'm sure. But that's enough dillydallying around. Time to chop some wood and bring in water, then we'll eat."

Always the taskmaster, her grandmother could never talk for more than five minutes, never divulge any of the information about her parents that Emily so longed to hear.

After dinner, which Emily could barely swallow, she and Luke went to the parlor to talk. Now that he had made his intentions known, it was permissible to be alone, if someone was nearby. Her grandparents were in the dining room around the wood stove, as they were each evening.

Luke stood beside the open doorway as Emily entered. It was strange, but she had never noticed how oppressive the room was before. The heavy drapes were drawn and the room smelled musty, and had ever since the tree had been removed.

Luke sat on one end of the sofa while Emily sat in the willow rocker usually occupied by Grandmother.

"I spoke of my intentions today."

"I know. Grandmother told me."

"I intended to wait, but started thinking about it. I need you now, Emily."

She looked into his face. His eyes were warm; kind. She nodded before looking away.

"I think of thee as a brother, Luke. I realized it even more this evening when I saw your buggy in the driveway." Emily raised her eyes to his. "I was excited about your being here, but not in the way you might wish. I think of you as a friend whom I can talk to freely."

"I understand that, Emily, and there is certainly nothing wrong with that."

"You spoke of love the other day, saying it isn't as important as people think it is, yet you loved your wife. You still love her, or so you said that First Day when we talked here in the parlor."

"Yes, that is true."

"Do you really think one should settle for less?"

"It depends on the circumstances." Luke rose and walked over to Emily. "Is there someone else?"

"I. . .met a man. He's a friend of Kate's, and I try to tell myself I do not care, that it isn't right, that he isn't a man of God."

"Yet he is still in your heart."

She nodded, saying nothing.

"Love is a strange thing, Emily. I know it to be so. Here I buried Rachel nearly a year ago, yet cannot wrench her from my mind. She is in my thoughts constantly, and that is why I could not profess my love for you. 'Twould not be honest."

"Nor I to you," Emily said, lifting her face.

"Does thee think we could eventually get over our hurts?"

Emily didn't have the answer. Luke's wife was gone to him forever, but it wasn't the same for Emily as Ben was very much alive. Time heals all wounds, but if God didn't take away the memory, how could she get over him?

"Your silence has told me what I need to know," Luke said. "I will wait to make the announcement, Emily. And now I must go."

"No. Wait." Emily called as he got to the door. "I know it is what God wants me to do, and I want you to come calling."

"Emily." He took her hands and held them to his face. "You have made me exceedingly happy tonight."

Long after Luke had gone, Emily thought about how he had held her hands. "God be with you, with us," were his parting words. That night she had much to write in the diary.

fourteen

Kate wore her new blue gingham on Friday. She'd spent the last two evenings sewing it on her new machine.

Her hair looked bouncier, Emily thought, and a smile crossed her face as she walked into the work area. "Kurt is coming by after work—"

"Kate!" Emily interrupted. "What has happened? You look somehow different."

"You'll know later."

"You said yes to his proposal."

Her dark eyes twinkled. "Maybe yes, maybe no."

Emily popped an imperfect chocolate into her mouth. She didn't like guessing games. "Quit talking so I can do my job right. Here's another lopsided coconut creme."

Kate set it aside. "If I'm to wear my best dress, I must cut out eating so much.

Emily knew it was true. Kurt had won Kate over. They would marry. Maybe they would marry before she and Luke.

"I want to come. Am I invited?"

Kate rolled her eyes. "Silly thing. Of course you're invited. You can stand up with me as a witness."

The rest of the day flew by. Not once did Emily think about Luke, what marriage to him would entail, whether they might grow to love one another, and eventually have a child. For now she was happy for Kate.

"When is the date?"

Kate looked toward the ceiling. "One doesn't decide

these things so quickly."

"What will you wear? Probably a new dress. With that sewing machine, you can make one in a week." Emily could picture Kate in a flowing dress made of palest pink or a soft cream. Since Kate had been married before, it wouldn't be appropriate to wear white.

"I want you to wear the blue velvet," Kate said. "I'll wear whatever goes with the velvet."

Emily wished Kate hadn't brought up the blue velvet dress. She had tried to forget about the dress, the way it had fit, the way she had felt like a princess, as she was swept off across the dance floor, waltzing to the "The Blue Danube Waltz." When she was old and her brow was furrowed with hundreds of lines, she would remember that special night. Thank God for memories—for giving her a night to recall.

"You're daydreaming again," Kate broke into her thoughts. "What are you thinking about this time?"

Emily shrugged, trying not to let the color flood her cheeks as it did when she thought about Ben. "Thinking how beautiful of a bride you will be."

"Not any prettier than you," Kate said. "I can't wait to be at your wedding."

Emily stopped dipping. "Oh, I don't think it will be that big of an occasion. I mean, Luke's been married before. The Friends don't believe in much fanfare, you know."

"That's a shame," Kate said. "I think all marriages should be fancy and cost lots of money." Her eyes twinkled with mischief so Emily knew she didn't mean it.

"Luke said we might take the streetcar down to Broadway and have dinner at the Benson Hotel. I understand it's the best place in town."

"How wonderful," Kate said, but her voice sounded

almost sarcastic.

"Kurt will insist on giving you a ride home," Kate said then. "He is very fond of you, you know."

"Fond of me? But, why? I've scarcely spoken more than two words to him."

"He just likes you, that's all."

Emily was pondering about that when Mr. Roberts walked up. "Emily, we're trying a new candy making technique and I'd like you to learn it. Would you come with me, please?"

She ended up in another part of the factory while Kate stayed in their usual work space. She liked learning new things, but she didn't like working alone. She missed chatting with Kate. Still, they could eat lunch together, so that was something.

At five, close to quitting time, Mr. Roberts popped in, saying there was someone to see her. "He's in the waiting area."

Emily wondered who it could be as she washed and dried her hands. Had Luke stopped by for some reason? He had once before and had taken her home. She removed the hairnet and patted her hair into place.

She saw the back, the wool overcoat, and boots and her heart stood still. *Ben. Oh, my. . .* It was Ben Galloway. A little gasp escaped from her mouth.

He turned and in a second, she was in his arms, pressed tight against his chest, tears forming in her eyes, spilling down her cheeks. It happened so fast, she couldn't believe she had fallen into his arms like that, and her a betrothed woman.

"Emily, oh, my darling, I've missed you so!"

He held her at arm's length, studying her face, her hair, her whole being, then he pulled her to him again. "I never knew how much I cared until I looked up and saw your face, the surprise in your eyes. That look told me everything I had asked myself a thousand times since I left Oregon, while I was in Iowa, and on my way back home."

Emily pulled away. "Ben, I'm sorry, but there's something you must know." Her heart twisted inside her as she looked away from his solid gaze. "I'm betrothed to Pastor Luke Morrison. I mentioned him before you left. . ."

"Yes, you did. And why do you suppose I left Iowa so quickly?" He pulled her back to him. "Why did I give up getting a better price for the house, the property?"

"But, you shouldn't have. Not on account of me." She found herself sinking into the look on his face, the dear, precious face she had memorized, the face that haunted her thoughts every waking hour.

"I love you, Emily, and so help me I know it's wrong to make a declaration like this without first going to your grandfather, but I've loved you since that night we danced. No, I knew it before I danced with you." He cupped her chin in his hand, forcing her to look into his eyes. "I'm going about this the wrong way. I'm frightening you to be saying all this. I know the protocol, but seeing you again after all these weeks, and I lost myself. I sort of—" he paused for a long moment, his eyes never leaving her face, "imagined, or at least hoped you felt the same way."

She wanted to be held tightly against him. She couldn't still her pounding heart, nor could she make her legs even move, though she knew the best thing she could do would be to turn and run as fast as she could. People didn't fall in love after one meeting. *No.* God hadn't intended for that to happen. She knew it wasn't right.

"Miss Drake," Mr. Roberts said, suddenly appearing in the waiting room. "Why don't you take off for the rest of the day? I think you've had enough training for one day."

The inner door opened and suddenly Kate was there,

squealing with delight at the sight of Ben.

"Ben! I knew you'd come soon. I just knew it!"

Emily whirled. "You mean you knew he was coming today?"

"Not today." Kate's eyes teased. "Sometime this week, I hoped."

Emily realized that it wasn't Kurt, but Ben that was coming, and Kate had wanted to surprise her.

"I want you to meet my family, Ma and Pearl," Ben said. "I don't want to wait until Saturday, but will if I must. Kate can come along as chaperone."

Emily longed to, but how could she? It wasn't proper to be seen with Ben when she had more or less said yes to Luke's proposal. True it wasn't a proposal in the usual sense, but he was proposing marriage, and they would live together as man and wife in name only. No one else was to know this part, and it had been difficult, but she hadn't told Kate that part. What if someone saw her with Ben? What might her grandparents and others say? It wasn't right.

"I can't," she murmured.

"You're going to marry a man you don't love," Ben said, taking Emily's hand. She didn't pull away.

"You love me, but you can't marry me."

They stepped out into the late March afternoon. The earlier showers had given way to sunshine, and it felt good on Emily's shoulders and back.

"You know why. I explained it before you left for Iowa."

"I know, but it didn't make sense then and makes even less sense now. How can you marry a man you do not love?"

"I will grow to love him."

Kate walked up, handing Emily her coat, hat, and gloves. "Ben, I've tried, so help me I have, but her mind is made up. It's the church thing."

Ben squared his shoulders, his voice shouting over the din of two passing carriages. "I won't let it happen," he yelled. "I simply will not."

Emily stepped back, saying nothing.

"I know what we should do," Kate said. "There's that new emporium on Woodstock. Let's go have a soda and talk some more. I've been dying to see what all they have. It's a huge place with all sorts of merchandise."

Always the one for adventure, Kate looked at Ben expectantly.

"Sounds wonderful, Kate. I heard about it before I left for Iowa."

Emily finally agreed to accompany Ben and Kate to the emporium where they ordered sodas. They found a table at the back and Emily slid in a booth, across from Kate. Ben sat next to her. Aware of his presence, she wondered if she could swallow. When she glanced at Ben for a brief moment, it was all she could do to keep from reaching out and touching him.

"I'll come to church on Sunday," Ben said, stirring his soda with a straw. "I will announce my intentions to your preacher after the meeting."

Emily touched his arm. "You can't. Oh, Ben, you can't."

"And why not?" He studied her face, his eyebrows knitting together in a frown.

Emily didn't quite know how to answer. "It would be awkward."

Ben shrugged. "For whom? You or this Luke?"

"For everyone," Emily said in a soft whisper.

"I told you I would attend your church, promised to let our children be raised in your faith. I—"

She heard no more. *Children.* Sudden tears filled her eyes at the thought of a child filling her womb.

"Here, now don't start crying." Ben removed a clean white handkerchief from his pocket, brushing Emily's tears away.

"I think it's the best idea," Kate said. "It certainly wouldn't be the first time two men fought for a woman's hand. Why shouldn't Luke know that someone else finds Emily desirable?"

Emily didn't know what to do or say. What would happen if Ben came to church and spoke to Luke about her? What would Luke do? Worse yet, how would her grandparents react?

"How is your mother and sister?" Kate asked, as if trying to change the subject.

"Fine. They're staying on the property, in the little cabin until the big house is finished. It's been too wet for my partner to do much while I was gone." He turned and looked into Emily's eyes again. "I don't want to wait, Emily. I want to court you as soon as possible."

Emily said nothing. She shouldn't have promised Luke she'd marry him. She knew she could never go through with the vows, not the way she was feeling now. She had honestly thought it would work, but it wouldn't be fair to him. Kate had been right all along. It wouldn't be right to marry Ben, either. She would try to go back to how it all was before. She'd be a spinster. Life was less complicated that way.

"You're too quiet," Ben said, taking her hand again, lifting it to his lips.

Trembling, Emily pulled back. She couldn't believe Ben had done that. She had no business marrying Luke or Ben. The sudden thought surprised her. Of course. It was the answer, or at least one answer. If she didn't marry either man, her life would be smooth once again. Ben would find someone more to his liking, one who loved dancing and could help him build his house on the hill in Oregon City. Not marrying Luke, freed him up for another lady in the Friends' Church. There were no single, young women right now, but the meeting was growing, and with his dedicated heart and kind manner, there would be someone. She knew this was so. It was all a matter of time.

"I cannot see you," Emily said finally.

"I can wait. If I have to."

It was now Emily's turn to be surprised. She hadn't expected that response.

She shook her head. "It will alleviate all problems if I don't marry anyone."

"Oh, no." Ben looked at Kate, as if he expected her to help plead his case.

"That's ridiculous, Emily," Kate said. "You'd be punishing yourself and for what reason?"

"Because it isn't meant to be."

"I don't believe that," Kate replied.

"It's easier this way."

"Yes, maybe so, for you." A pained expression crossed Ben's face. "Your suggested solution is not the answer, however."

They left the emporium, and Emily paused. "Thank you for the soda. It was the first I ever had."

"I have something else for you," Ben said, leaning over and pulling a small package out from under a buggy cushion. He handed it to her.

"For me?" Emily frowned. "But, why are you giving me another gift?"

"Just open it," Kate said. "I love surprises."

Emily fumbled with the string, and slid off the plain brown wrapping paper. It was a book. She gasped as she touched the blue cover.

"*Leaves of Grass* by Walt Whitman," she read aloud. She opened the page and read the inscription on the inside page.

> *To Emily, who likes to read.*
> *With Love from Ben Galloway.*

"Oh," she gasped again. "It's *beautiful*. I've never owned a book before."

"I know," Ben said, his hand touching her shoulder. "And that's why when I saw it in this store, I knew it was the best gift of all."

Sudden tears filled her eyes. "It's not the best gift," she said then. "My Black Beauty is the best gift."

"Black Beauty?" He grinned. "The little horse I carved for you is Black Beauty?"

"Yes, it seemed the right name."

Kate touched the book. "This is so nice, Ben. I didn't know you liked poetry."

Ben shrugged. "I don't know if I do or not, but thought Emily might read me some of it."

He had known it was the perfect gift, but hadn't realized how much it would mean to her. He watched as her fingers touched the cover, and felt the pages and how her eyes skimmed over the first few pages. Yes, it had been the right choice. When he heard that Whitman was a Quaker, he knew that made it even more special. Now if he could bring the smile back to her face when she looked at him. If he could make her forget what she thought she was supposed to do and follow her heart, he would be happy. He was as confident as ever that she cared for him deeply. If only he could convince her of that.

Emily jumped suddenly. "I really must get home. It's terribly late."

"It's off to home then," Ben said, giving Emily a lift into the buggy. Kate had already climbed into the back and sat, waiting for the horses to start.

"I haven't seen Black Beauty," Kate said to Emily. "Bring him to work one day."

"Soon she will have one to match," said Ben, "except the colt is a light brown with a white star on its forehead.

"I simply cannot accept another gift," Emily said, glancing at Ben. "You have given me too much already."

"I don't think so." Their eyes met and her face flushed. She turned away.

"It's isn't proper," she insisted.

"There doesn't need to be a reason to give a gift," Kate said. "I'd certainly never turn down one."

"I agree," Ben said, looking at Emily.

Emily didn't know what to say, so said nothing, until they arrived at the end of the road and she had to get out.

"Please let me off at the corner," she said, touching Ben's arm. "I'll walk the rest of the way."

"I don't like any of this," Ben said. "We need to discuss our situation. I'd like to meet your grandparents, tell them my intentions and go from there." His face was stern.

Emily felt panicky. "No! It can't be that way. Please understand. I have been spoken for."

"I came as soon as possible after receiving Kate's letter. I must speak to your grandfather," he fairly thundered, his eyes shooting sparks in her direction.

"Kate's letter?" She looked stunned.

Kate stammered, "Yes, I wrote Ben a letter—"

"And I wrote to you, Emily," Ben broke in. "Sent it to Kate's house."

Now it was Kate's turn to look stunned. "You did? I never received it."

"I know I mailed it. I thought I had the right address."

It was too late for letters, Emily thought, not that it would have changed anything.

"I want to meet your grandfather," Ben said, more insistent.

"No!" Emily jumped down. "I cannot see you anymore, Ben Galloway. You don't. . .you can't mean anything to me." The minute the words were said and she saw the look on his face, she wanted to take them back.

"Very well, then. I'll let you off here, and do as you wish." His voice sounded controlled. Firm. Emily thought she detected anger, or was it hurt?

The buggy turned the corner, and she realized with a sinking sensation what she had done, how her words had stung. If only she could see once more his look of longing. If only she could have run after him, if only she could have said his name, and felt him reach down for her, pulling her close again. She never wanted to forget that feeling. She never wanted to forget the way Ben had looked at her earlier, before the anger. But the look of hurt and disbelief was repressed from her memory. It would be easier that way.

She lifted her skirts, stepped over a mud puddle and made her way down the lane to the house. If she was lucky, Grandmother wouldn't have much to say. If she was lucky, she could go out, do her chores, then come in to a quiet supper. If she was lucky, she could soon forget this day had ever happened. If she was lucky, she would soon forget Ben Galloway, his eyes, his touch, and most of all that incredibly bushy hair.

fifteen

Luke came to the factory to pick up Emily on Thursday the next week. Kate had just caught the streetcar, so did not meet him. She had been distant since Ben's return.

As Luke and Emily drove over the miles to the farmhouse, her mind went from thoughts of Ben and how he had looked before driving off, to thoughts of Luke and how right and good marriage to him would be.

"Have you thought about setting a date?" he asked. "Would a June wedding be pushing it too much?"

"I don't know." Emily stared straight ahead. "It is such a —commitment—and I. . .I don't think I'm ready to marry anyone."

"If there are still doubts, it would be wrong. When does thee think thee will be ready?"

Emily thought about what it would be like to have her own home. Cooking her own meals. Sewing. Ironing. Washing clothes. Doing what she wanted when she wanted sounded wonderful. No Grandmother peering over her shoulder telling her she had put too much salt in the pot of beans or hadn't sliced the bread thin enough. Emily felt like such a child when Grandmother was around—always had.

And work. She would quit work as no wife worked unless she was a widow. There would be plenty for a preacher's wife to do. Luke would need her in many ways.

It was tempting. Very much so. Still, she could not get Ben's face out of her mind, her thoughts. As long as she thought of him, it would not be fair to Luke, even if he didn't love her. How could she sit across the table each morning, each night and do for him when she wished he was another man?

"I understand your hesitancy," Luke said as he rose and walked across the room. "Once vows are repeated, one cannot change one's mind."

The air was warm, the sun, a bright red circle setting behind them. Emily turned to look at the sunset.

"It's this fellow, isn't it, Emily?"

She could feel his eyes on her, but she didn't dare look in his direction. She could say no, but she could not lie, especially not to Luke.

"Does he believe in God?"

Emily nodded. "He says he does."

"And do you believe him?"

Sudden tears gathered in her eyes. "Yes."

"I see." Luke sat back, fingering his beard. "You still care, that is obvious."

"I try to tell myself I do not care. . .that it isn't right."

"But it is there, burning inside you, making you experience doubts."

Emily didn't know how to answer. The thought that continued to torment her was the look in Ben's eyes when she said he didn't mean anything to her. It had been a lie, and just as she could not lie to Luke, why had she thought it was all right to lie to Ben?

"We must wait a while longer."

"Yes." Emily glanced over now. "I can talk with thee so much easier than most people. It is a special feeling I have for thee, but more like I would to a brother." There. She'd finally admitted how she felt. What would he say now?

Luke nodded. "I understand that feeling, Emily. I

happen to believe we could make a wonderful home, serve our church, our community well, but God wants it to be right for both of us."

"My grandparents, they will not understand."

"Thee is right. They will not understand. It's going to be hard for them. They want you to be happy, to have a home provided for you. Thee may not think that, but I know it is so."

"I cannot stay with them any longer, Luke. Kate has invited me to live with her, and I think that is the best decision for me now."

"Yes, this may be good." He reached over, touching her shoulder. "You need to try your own wings. There's a wonderful life ahead of you, Emily. Maybe it's time you found out what it is."

Emily lifted her face to the sky. "What you said makes me think of my favorite verse—"

"Don't tell me, let me guess." He looked upward too, reciting the familiar passage: "'But they that wait upon the Lord shall renew their strength; they shall mount up with wings as eagles; they shall run, and not be weary, and they shall walk, and not faint.'" (Isaiah 40:31)

 る

Later Emily couldn't believe Luke had understood her feelings. Long after he had gone—and she'd had to make excuses for his not coming in—she sat in the dimness of the dining room, warming herself by the fire. She marveled at how freely they could talk. It was not that way with Ben. Did love have something to do with it? Emily could talk to Luke because she did not love him. Luke could talk to Emily because he did not love her. Love seemed to complicate, to confuse things. Did she *really* know what she was doing? What was God's answer in all this?

Marriage seemed wrong for now. The confusion encompassed her, making her full of doubts. Waiting was the only way.

Emily sat, considering her options. Her grandparents would be horrified if she moved out, if she decided not to marry Luke. They would not understand. The ramifications were there, and there were things she could not take lightly. Yet wasn't it time to try her wings? To begin making her own decisions? Time to try her wings. It was good advice and it came from her pastor. How could anyone argue with that?

She would not tell Grandmother, not yet. She wasn't strong enough to match the volley of words that would most definitely come her way. She'd pack her clothes and wraps, the diary, the book of poems, and the first quilt she had ever made. Black Beauty would be in her pocket and the silver hair clasp. That was all. Kate had extra bedding and a four poster in her spare room. Nothing else was needed.

Emily went up the stairs. It was quite late, but she knew she wouldn't sleep. She glanced at the quilt. Strangely enough it was the wedding ring design and had been the first one she had made. Her hand ran over the tiny stitches as the memory filled her. It had taken so long, and she'd had to rip out some of the stitches since Grandmother was particular. Surely Grandmother would want her to have it.

She undid her braid and slowly unwound it, letting the brown hair fall about her shoulders. Taking a brush, she brushed until the tangles were gone, then kept brushing as her mind thought over the years, all that had happened since she came to stay with her grandparents. She'd been such a lost, frightened little girl. She had cried herself to sleep many nights, wondering what everyone was doing back home, wishing she could hug her mother once more, listen to her father's happy notes on the violin, feel Mary's arm flinging across the bed, hitting her in the nose. And Maud. Maud who tossed and turned a lot, talking in her sleep. She'd even been known to wet the bed.

There'd been nobody here, no one to turn to, nobody to hug, nobody to cuddle up to and she had nearly died from the loneliness.

A small mirror on the wall showed her now, a young woman with lean body, hair half way down her back. Eyes a deep blue, a small bosom, but a nice nose and full lips. Her cheeks were pink from being close to the downstairs fire, but also because of the decision Luke had helped her make. She was giving up both men. She'd go back to being a spinster. Life was less complicationed that way.

She opened the diary. Writing in tiny script, saving every last page, every bit of margin until there was no more room, she knew she would buy another book, something else to put her thoughts in. Sometimes she felt writing had been her salvation. It had helped her get through day after day when she felt nobody loved or cared about her. She knew God cared, but He wasn't tangible.

Mama,
I'm moving to Kate's. I need to think about what is right in my life. I love you Mama. . .I always have.

"Oh, God." Emily fell to her knees. "Is it wrong what I am about to do? Is it a selfish desire? I still feel Your hand in my life, feel Your presence even now in this room, know that You are with me because You promised to love me always."

She looked around the room at the pale walls. Once they had been pink, but were faded from time. She could not take her few belongings on the streetcar. Perhaps Kurt could come with Kate after work. Emily opened her book of poetry, her gift from Ben. She had read the poems so many times, she had memorized them. How had Ben known she had always wanted a book of her very own?

O Captain! my Captain! our fearful trip is done;
The ship has weather'd every rack, the prize we
  sought is won;
The port is near, the bells I hear, the people all
  exulting,
While follow eyes the steady keel, the vessel dim
  and daring:
But, O heart! heart! heart!
O, the bleeding drops of red.
Where on the deck my Captain lies
Fallen cold and dead.

Tears filled her eyes as she recited the poem word for word. Reaching back into the drawer, she grasped Black Beauty, holding him to her cheek. She loved the maker, but the manner in which they had met had been wrong. Someday she could forget him, but never would she forget the night at the dance, the kiss on her cheek or how it had felt to be engulfed in his arms when he'd returned from Iowa. And the horse. He had worked on it and even said there was a colt he had made to go with Black Beauty. Of course she could not accept it now. Not after the angry words, the misunderstandings. It was just as well, she knew.

sixteen

Kate was ecstatic the next morning when Emily told her about her decision.

Her face lit up. "You're moving in with me and *not* marrying Luke?"

Emily nodded. "I cannot and he understood."

"He did?" Kate stared open-mouthed.

"Yes. He was nice about it, Kate, said he knew how I felt."

"Emily, I take back all the things I said about him. He must be a very special person."

Emily nodded. "He is, Kate, and he plans to speak with Grandmother and Grandfather about my leaving, help ease the loss."

"How are you getting out of there without causing trouble? I doubt that your grandmother is going to just smile and let it go at that."

Emily shook her head. "I know. That's the part that worries me." Grandmother would say things, sharp, hurting words, and she might crumble under the attack.

Kate touched her shoulder. "Kurt is coming by after work and I'll ask him about picking up your things."

"Would Saturday be all right?" It would take until then for her to work up her courage.

"I'm sure it will be fine."

Emily felt like singing all day. Her heart was light, her mind whirling with exciting thoughts. It would be good to be on her own for the first time ever. Kate might not stay single. Kurt might come to mean more at some time in the future, but for the present, she would make a home with her good friend. She could try to rebuild her life, decide what was best. If her grandparents did not understand why she had to do this, so be it. She would cross that bridge when she came to it. For now she knew she was doing the right thing for her. For Luke. And for Ben, too.

Ben. He would probably always be in her heart, she realized now. It would be, indeed, difficult to get over him, but God could show her the way. Learning to do things for herself was a step in the right direction. She felt better about her decision already. Funny how one decision could free her up like this. She would soar on eagle's wings. She would run and not be weary, walk and not be faint. Yes, thank God, she was on her way.

❧

When Kurt arrived on Saturday, Emily steeled herself. She knew she should have told Grandmother ahead of time that she was moving out. If only she could have talked to her once, let her know how she felt about things, that she was no longer a little girl but a woman who should be able to make decisions on her own.

The knock sounded and a minute later Kurt entered the farmhouse, hat in hand. "I've come to help Miss Emily."

"Help?" Grandmother asked, a puzzled look on her weathered face. "What on earth is thee speaking of?"

Emily entered the room. "I'm moving to Kate's, Grandmother."

She knew she would remember that look for as long as she lived. The questioning, disbelief, then anger.

"Thee surely couldn't have thought this out."

"I have, Grandmother."

"Thee doesn't appreciate all we've done for thee." Her voice rose and Grandfather hobbled into the room.

"What is wrong? Emily?"

"She's moving out into an unchaperoned home where who knows what will happen. Does Pastor Luke know about this?"

"He does." Emily started up the stairs, lifting her skirts as she went. It would take two trips to carry her valise and the rest of her belongings. Grandmother was going on about the "younger generation" and how they didn't know anything or have respect. Emily grabbed her few possessions and went down the stairs.

Kurt stood, hat in hand, and took the valise from her hand.

"Nice meeting you," he said, but of course neither grandparent responded.

She had done it. Tears filled her eyes as she rode over the miles to Kate's house. There were many things she wanted to say, hugs for Grandfather, but she couldn't. It would have been wrong and to stay would have meant more verbal accusations. This was the way it had to be. A clean break.

&

At last they reached their destination and Kate ran out to hug Emily. "I can see you've been crying, but it's going to work out. I know God has plans for you, dear friend."

Kate had fixed up the spare room for Emily. Blue gingham curtains, made from the scraps from Kate's dress and with her new sewing machine, hung at the windows.

"Your new dress is in the closet," Kate said, opening the door.

Emily stared at the pink lawn material with ruffles at the collar and one deep ruffle at the hem line. Ruffles. She'd never had ruffles before and loved them at first sight.

"Kate, it's just too much. The dress is beautiful, the room is beautiful, and how can I ever thank you?"

"By being my friend," Kate said. "That's all the payment I'll ever ask."

"I can give you some out of my pay check each week."

"You certainly will not," Kate interjected. "I won't accept it. I want you to start saving to make the train trip to California."

California. Emily's mind raced at the thought. Was she really going to go after all these years? What would her mother say? *And Papa?* She wouldn't even recognize them, she knew, just as they wouldn't recognize her. Too many years had gone by.

Kate held her hands behind her back and suddenly thrust something under Emily's nose.

"It's a Teddy bear, named after the President of the United States. Isn't he cute? He's yours to remind you that you are loved and cherished."

Tears welled up in Emily's eyes. She'd never owned toys, except for one doll when she was very young.

Emily placed the wedding ring quilt at the foot of the bed. Kate already had blankets on it, but her own quilt would add color to the room and a welcome bit of familiarity.

Emily hung up her gray dress, right next to the pink lawn, and her undergarments went into the chest of drawers. There wasn't much to put away. She set her Bible, then the diary on the night stand, then next to that, the book of poems Ben had given her. Her treasures.

"Come," Kate said from the doorway. "Have a cup of tea. Rest for a minute. You must be tired."

Emily sipped her tea and wondered if she should pinch herself. How could this be happening? It didn't seem possible. Soon she would waken and discover it all a dream. She would be back at her grandparents', fetching water or setting the table for dinner.

"It's going to be wonderful having you here," Kate said, her eyes watching Emily. "You're the sister I never had."

"And you're the sister I had to give up," Emily answered. "I am?"

Kate giggled and soon Emily was giggling. She hadn't giggled, for many, many years, and she didn't even know what she was giggling about now. Nothing was funny. Still one sip of her tea, a glance in Kate's direction, and she started giggling again. It was a good, wonderful feeling, one she hadn't experienced since leaving her parents. She vaguely recalled giggling under the bed covers with Mary and Maud, trying to be quiet so Ma wouldn't scold.

The next few weeks were more precious than any Emily could remember. She and Kate went to work six mornings a week, came home and fixed a simple supper. They read books since Emily took the streetcar to the library one Saturday and checked out the limit. Some evenings they worked on sewing, embroidery, or darning. Emily baked the bread and churned the cream into butter, because she liked to, not because she had to. Sometimes she'd think about Grandfather, wondering how he was doing, hoping Grandmother was being kind. And sometimes she'd think about Ben. She tried not to, but he was there in her innermost thoughts. And the blue velvet dress hanging in her closet was a constant reminder. She also thought about Luke, hoping he would find a wife soon.

❧

Ben had never worked as hard as he did in those weeks after returning from Iowa. He tried not to think about Emily and the words she had flung at him after she'd jumped down from the buggy. Had she really meant what she said? That she did not think of him, that she had never cared?

He wanted to forget her. He tried to forget her, driving himself from sun-up until well after dark. The Oregon

City house was coming along well. It was a new bunga-low style with dormers and a good quality wood siding. Even now as Ben looked at it, he knew he would not be able to live there. It had been Emily's house, designed with her in mind, but he had discovered it was too far from most of his jobs. He needed to be closer to town. He started buying up lots on Foster, not far from Kate's. There was one nice lot, right on the streetcar line, that seemed perfect for a house. He had another set of plans drawn up. More bedrooms this time. He didn't know who he would marry, and right now he didn't even care. Maybe he could have one of those "prearranged" marriages, too. He'd been a bachelor long enough and it was past time to settle down.

Ma was happy in her new surroundings, and already had a garden planted, in between rain that is.

Pearl's cheeks had filled out and were rosy and pink. She liked school. She helped in the afternoons after get-ting home and soon the garden was flourishing. Ben went out on Sundays to visit, but the rest of the week he stayed in at the boarding house where he'd first lived when com-ing to Portland. He hired a man to help with the framing while he did the finishing work. He would always have cabinets to build since he was particular about the mea-surements, and his name was in demand.

"I've never seen such fine work," Mr. Talbot had said before Ben left for Iowa. Ben, alone, could keep busy with more work than he could handle. He now left most of the building up to John Creel and the new hired young man. John was honest and forthright and worked hard.

Still, Ben's heart ached. He attended the dances at the grange and heard about another dance and a special music concert held at Canemah Park. It was on Sundays and he took Pearl one Sunday to hear the music. Dressed in a calico with her hair pinned up, she looked older than fourteen.

Ben looked out over the crowd, looking for Emily. Always looking, always thinking about Emily. Once when he'd danced with Kate, she said to be patient, that Emily wasn't sure what she wanted.

Patient. He had never been patient about waiting to see what God had in mind, and how could he be sure that his life would ever be in order? Once again he found himself thinking about the verse in Romans: *And we know that all things work together for good to them that love God, to them who are called according to his purpose.* (Romans 8:28)

As the house on Foster neared completion, Ben worked evenings on the cabinets. The electricity was hooked up, so there was no reason he couldn't work after dark. There was indoor plumbing and he planned to put in a telephone once he moved in.

He looked around the vacant house, thinking again how much he needed someone to help fill the rooms. A wife. Children. He surveyed one room longer. It looked out on the back side at a forested area. They were in town, but because he had left several trees, the lot retained its desirability. The room that was originally to be a bedroom now made him think of a study. Yes. Why not? He would build shelves along one entire wall, enough shelves to hold hundreds of books.

When he saw his mother that Sunday, she told him to sit, to relax while she fixed him a hot noon meal. "You're looking peaked these days, son. You're working too hard, and all for naught."

"It isn't for naught," he said, running a hand through his bushy hair. "Nothing is ever for naught."

"I know why you're doing it, and I think it's time to forget and to go on. One cannot wait forever."

His mother, so dear to him, sat sipping her tea, rocking

in the chair that had finally arrived from Iowa.

"Ma, I know you're worried, but don't be. I'm going to be fine. Hard work never hurt a soul."

"I pray you know what you are doing."

He knew what he was doing, all right. He was trying to get over a broken heart. He was trying to forget a pair of deep blue eyes and a shy smile and eyes that gazed with meaning into his own. *Forget? Give up? Never.*

He left and made it back to the boarding house well after dark, but he was singing a song, humming the "Blue Danube Waltz."

❧

It was the following Saturday he saw Kate and she told him the news that Emily was not working for the pastor anymore. She wasn't living with her grandparents and that bit of news shocked him. Could it be true? He knew, as he had always known, that fear was what drove Emily. Fear of her grandparents' wrath. She didn't do anything that did not meet with their approval. He couldn't understand it. Kate had said she left her family in California years ago and had come to live with the grandparents. Why were they cruel? Ben had never known anything but love in his family. He had always assumed that that was the way it was.

A thin shred of expectation built inside him after that night and he felt a renewal of optimism. Emily wasn't as far out of reach as she had once been. Yes, God had opened the door just a crack and Ben was going to make certain it didn't slam again.

seventeen

Pastor Luke came visiting the week after Emily moved to Kate's. He had agreed that it would be better if Emily didn't come to work for him.

Kate answered the door, and stared at the short, intense man standing on her porch.

He took off his hat. "I'm Pastor Luke Morrison. And you must be—"

"Katherine Russell." She extended her hand. "I'm so glad we finally get to meet. Come in, come in. Goodness where are my manners?"

Luke smiled. "Yes, I've certainly heard a lot about you through Emily. Is she here?"

Emily appeared around the corner, wiping hands on her apron. She'd been making muffins, and a smudge of flour graced the tip of her nose.

"Pastor Luke, how nice of you to stop by." She had feared she might feel awkward around him, but one look at his smile and she relaxed.

"I've just finished the baking and the water is hot for tea. Would you like a cup?"

Kate, never the quiet one, nodded. "Oh, yes, do please come sit down."

"I'd take you to the parlor," Emily said, "but the parlor is now the sewing room. The kitchen is much warmer, anyway."

"Well, my goodness, I guess I could at least offer to take your coat, Reverend." Kate seemed flustered.

"Yes, to all things," Luke finally answered. "I have time for tea, I much prefer the kitchen, and yes, please, thank you for taking my coat and hat." He smiled in Kate's direction.

He handed Emily a small envelope. "From your grandparents. Your money. They said they wouldn't take it. I'm sorry they feel that way."

She sighed and pulled out a chair. "I suppose they have disinherited me."

"Maybe they will get over it," Luke said. "Give it time, Emily."

"You don't know Grandmother. She will never get over it. She'll carry her hurt and anger to the grave."

Kate placed cups in front of them and sat at the far end of the table. "I hope you don't mind if I sit in on this conversation."

"No, by all means, do join us," Luke said.

"I was thinking you might want to pray with us and perhaps read some scripture," Kate said then. "I know Emily misses church. I just wish I had a piano for her to play here."

Luke's eyes showed surprise at Kate's suggestion. "I'm happy to hear your request for prayer and scripture reading, and am most happy to oblige."

"I have a few questions to ask," Kate said, setting her cup down. "I believe in God, but my God seems to be different from Emily's and your God."

"How so?" asked Luke.

Emily said nothing but stared into her nearly empty cup of tea.

"I believe that God is a God of love."

Luke leaned forward, flexing his fingers. "We Friends believe that, also."

"If that's so. . ." Kate paused for a long moment, "why are there so many restrictions?"

"Restrictions?" Luke looked puzzled. "Could you expound on that a bit?"

"Such as dancing." Kate tossed her head. "I see nothing wrong with dancing."

Luke nodded, looking thoughtful. "I see what you're asking—is it all right if I call you Kate?"

"Oh, yes, please do."

Emily rose and put her cup in the sink. She was as surprised as Luke at her request.

"I'm sorry, Kate, but we do think it is so. Dancing is a worldly pleasure and we try to keep ourselves pure and whole for God."

"But David danced," Kate said, taking Emily's Bible and pointing to the scripture: "And David danced before the Lord with all his might. . . ." (2 Samuel 6:14)

Luke nodded. "This pleases me that you've been searching the scriptures. Emily, you're quite the proselytizer."

She sat again. "We read scripture together every evening."

"Well, Kate, to get back to your question, it was different then. David danced before the Lord. He did not dance with a woman in his arms—"

"And if he had?" Kate interrupted.

"It would have been wrong and God would have told him so."

"I'm having a problem with that," Kate said, signaling Emily for more water for tea.

"The very backbone of our doctrine teaches humility," Luke continued. Servanthood. Modesty. We feel we are yoked with Jesus, and thus believe in upholding the scriptures."

"Which also means 'thou shalt not wear color'?"

Kate stood and her lavender gingham with its layers of crinolines flounced out. Her cheeks were bright with their usual touch of rouge. "I wear bright colors, as you can see, because they make me happy. And," she pointed to her hair, "ribbons and combs to dress up my hair."

"And on you they do look lovely."

Emily could scarcely believe her ears and turned to see Kate flush scarlet.

"But God gave color to the birds, animals, and beasts. How about the wild flowers in the meadow? Why would He expect His people to be colorless?"

"It goes back to the humility, Kate. It isn't that it is one of the great commandments, but we Friends believe our strengths lie in God's Word, not in things and desires of the flesh." Luke nodded as he continued. "We believe we are humble instruments of God, and declare more to the world by refusing to enter battle. We live our lives happily, peacefully, and quite satisfactorily by showing that certain pleasures and daily pursuits are not necessary. Simplicity keeps our minds on the real reason God put us on this earth in the first place."

Kate raised an eyebrow. "Which is? Do go on, Pastor Luke."

"When Jesus came, He said there are only two commandments we need worry ourselves about—"

"Two?" Kate broke in. "What happened to the ten?"

"If we but follow these two, the others are taken care of automatically. It's recorded here in the tenth chapter of Luke, verse twenty-seven: 'Thou shalt love the Lord thy God with all thy heart, and with all thy soul, and with all thy strength, and with all thy mind; and thy neighbor as thyself.'"

Kate seemed impressed as she reread the passage. "Yes," she said, her eyes widening. "It makes complete sense. If we treat our neighbor right, we will not bear false witness, kill or covet, or any of the other things."

Emily broke into the conversation. "I'm beginning to prepare some supper. Won't you stay to eat with us, Pastor Luke?"

"Oh, yes, you must because there are more things I want to ask," Kate said.

"Very well. I shall stay for supper." His eyes twinkled. "Since you both insist."

"I need to know if God forgives us for our sins," Kate continued."

"Of course He does," Emily said, looking up from the potato she was slicing. "I've explained that."

"But, if He does, why would one not be happy and rejoice? Because I found in Philippians where it says, 'Rejoice in the Lord always.'" (Philippians 4:4)

Luke grinned bigger than before. "And so it does, Kate. Yes, Paul taught that."

Emily felt her heart sink. She knew what Kate was getting to now. She was referring to her and how she wasn't able to forget the words spoken to Ben in anger. Or how she couldn't put out of her mind the night she'd gone to the dance.

"We believe a person is forgiven if he truly repents and promises to sin no more."

"So," Kate went on, "if a person asked God to forgive him, it should be over."

Luke glanced at Emily, but she turned away from his gaze. "People are often misled by a passion of the moment. It's a weakness of the flesh. But we are only human and the person must also forgive himself. And that is why we believe in meetings, as we are mighty in number and uphold each other in daily prayer."

"I do believe that," Kate said.

"Do you love God, Kate?"

"Yes, Pastor Luke, I believe I do."

"Don't test God. Love Him with all your heart and soul, mind, and strength, as the scripture tells us, and everything will fall into place."

Emily stirred the potatoes, but she couldn't see for the tears crowding her eyes. *Everything will fall into place*, she repeated to herself. Why had she not remembered it? Yes, she had not been joyful. Her heart had been laden with guilt and remorse. It didn't take much to rid herself of the feeling.

Sighing, she moved the pan off the stove and fell to her knees. "I am the one Kate speaks of, Luke. It is I who has not felt like rejoicing. I need forgiveness for my moment of weakness. I also need to own up to my own feelings and get on with my life."

Emily had never in her entire life delivered such a speech. Her eyes brimming, she felt Luke's hand on her head as he knelt beside her and prayed.

Kate was on the other side, her arm around Emily's shoulder. And just as they had done last Saturday, giggling like two schoolgirls, now they cried together.

"I must ask for Ben's forgiveness," Emily said at the conclusion of the prayer. "I hurt him deeply. I know because I saw it in his eyes."

"Yes, that is what thee must do," Luke said, standing back up. "I think everything is going to work out for thee now."

The supper was simple fare with fried potatoes, leftover butter beans, and thick slices of bread.

Luke finished off the beans and potatoes, then pushed his chair back. "It's been wonderful seeing you again, Emily, and meeting you, Kate. I'm glad we had this time of prayer. And remember, you're always welcome in meeting."

After handing him his coat and hat, Kate walked him to the door while Emily cleared the table.

He paused, regarding Kate closely. "If you'd like, I could come again and we could talk more about God's Word."

"I think I'd like that."

Long after he had gone, Emily sat staring at her embroidery work. Kate was in the sewing room, making white pinafores to wear over their dresses. She had been more quiet than usual after Luke had gone. Emily wanted to ask her what she was thinking, but knew Kate would talk about it when she felt like it. Emily wondered if Kate would stop wearing her bright dresses and jewelry.

The prayers for forgiveness made her feel so light and free. Emily hadn't liked herself very much. And she certainly hadn't been truthful. But her new feeling of release nearly overwhelmed her.

"I like your Pastor Luke," Kate said as she emerged from the bedroom with both pinafores completed.

"I'm not surprised," Emily said. "I knew the first day that he was going to be a wonderful, warm person."

Emily took her pinafore and put it on over her brown dress. "This look nice, Kate. It's like an apron."

"I didn't tell you this earlier," Kate said, "because I didn't want you to get the wrong idea."

"About what?" Emily removed the pinafore.

"Kurt is leaving for Seattle next week. He has taken a job there, and doesn't plan to return."

"Kate! No!"

"It's okay, Emily. He asked me to accompany him— after we were married, of course—but I told him though I cared very much for him, like you, I could not marry a man I did not love."

Emily's eyes filled with tears. "It wasn't because I'm here, was it? Because I can move. I can find somewhere to stay."

"Emily I realize that. You have enough money now, with what Pastor Luke brought today, for your train ticket to Monterey. It wasn't you holding me back, but my own heart knew it wasn't right."

"Will he stop to say good-bye?"

Kate smiled. "As a matter of fact, he wants us to go for a Sunday drive and will be by early. Almost as soon as the sun is up. We have a long drive ahead of us."

"We do?"

"Yes, and I want you to bring plenty of wraps and some blankets, as mornings are cold though the afternoons are warming up nicely. I'll pack a lunch tonight."

Emily chose the pink dress, one of the first made on Kate's sewing machine. Kate selected a flowered chambray and her new navy blue cloche, and they both planned on wearing the new pinafores.

Emily thought again about what Luke had said about color. Did she dwell on her clothing too much now? Could it be true, that such things took one from thoughts of God and serving Him? She didn't want that to happen. She wanted to attend church again, but perhaps a different one. It would be difficult to sit with her grandparents in the Meeting. They would stare, especially Grandmother and it would be uncomfortable.

Where were Kurt and Kate going that would take all day? She'd asked, but Kate had said she would soon see.

Kate loved surprises and assumed that everyone else did, also.

Before blowing out the light, Emily scrawled a few lines in a letter she would soon mail to her parents.

> *Mama,*
>
> *It's getting closer now. I will come to see you and Papa, and I hope all my brothers and sisters are nearby—except for Tom, of course—unless you have had word from him. I truly pray you have.*
>
> *I know it will be such a lovely time together and I look forward to catching up on everything that has happened. I love you, Mama! Tell Papa I am eager to hear "The Arkansas Traveler." And if you have a piano, I will play music for you. I play much better than I used to. I send you best regards.*
>
> *Your loving daughter,*
Emily Drake

Emily set the letter aside and said her prayers. She thanked God for the forgiveness, and for the riddance of the pain she'd felt for so long. She also thanked Him for her friend Kate and for Luke's caring, gentle manner. She then said a special prayer for her grandmother and grandfather. Some day, she hoped, they would want to see her and speak to her again. Some day, she hoped they would forgive and Grandmother would not feel bitterness toward her. Until then, she would carry on in her new life, and continue to be thankful and confident she was in the Lord's will.

eighteen

Kurt arrived ten minutes early. After removing his hat, he called out, "Good morning. It's certainly a wonderful day for a ride in the country. A bit nippy, perhaps, but it's bound to warm up."

Both women had warm coats, hats, and gloves and Emily smoothed down the skirt of her pink dress. It was the first time she had worn it, and she didn't feel wrong for wearing a light color. She felt good inside, and had lifted praises to God for His provisions and promises.

Emily had not seen this part of town before, nor had she seen the Willamette River, since that day when she was ten and had arrived on the train. She breathed deeply of the cool, crisp air. Never had a day seemed more perfect, nor a Sunday so wonderful.

They traveled south, taking in the flowering cherry and apple trees. From where she sat, Emily studied her two friends, wishing Kurt wouldn't move to Seattle, knowing she would miss seeing him, and wondering if Kate was the reason for the change. If only things had been different, but, then, life was full of disappointments. She'd learned that early on.

They began climbing and Emily thought they would never get to the top of a huge hill. The area was wooded with very few houses in sight. A buggy passed them and Emily laughed when the driver doffed his hat and waved.

"Look back over your shoulder," Kate called out.

Emily did and the breath caught in her throat. Never

had she seen such a hill, such a sky that seemed to take over, and the river, blue and clear way below them. It was a beautiful view.

"Another half mile and we're there," Kurt said.

Emily wondered where they were going, but that was part of the surprise. She felt the little horse in her pocket. She liked to keep Black Beauty there. It made her think of Ben, made her remember that night, made her remember his face and the snapping eyes, made her wonder if she would ever see him again, wonder if he even wanted to see her.

And then they stopped. Emily peered around the corner and saw a large lot cleared. A foundation and siding was up and off in one corner sat a smaller house with smoke coming out the chimney.

"Yahoo! Anyone home?" Kurt called.

The door of the cabin opened and Emily froze. She'd recognize that stance anywhere. *Ben.* Even from here, she could see his thick shock of hair, remember how bushy the eyebrows were, and her heart wouldn't stop pounding so hard.

"Come on in. Meet my family!"

Emily's fingers tightened on the collar of her coat. Would he know she had come, too? He couldn't see her in the back like this. She reached up and tugged on Kate. "Why didn't you tell me this was where we were coming?"

"Because you wouldn't have come, that's why," Kate retorted.

"You're right. Probably I would have protested. Still I do need to apologize."

"Ben has wanted me to meet his mother and sister, and I thought you should meet them, too."

So she was going to see Ben again. What might he say

to her, or she to him? She felt uncomfortable, but there was no place to hide.

The horse rode over the deep rutted land, threatening to bog down. "This wouldn't be so bad if it hadn't poured last night," Kurt said.

And then they were there and Ben walked up to the buggy.

"Kate! Kurt! I am so glad you both came. Ma and Pearl have wanted to meet some people. This is splendid—" his voice cut off in mid-sentence as his eyes suddenly focused on Emily.

"I. . .didn't know you brought someone."

"Ben, I want you to meet Emily. She's staying with me and I could hardly leave her home, now could I?"

Emily's cheeks flushed at the game the two were playing. Pretending that Ben didn't know her.

She extended her hands. Well, two could play this game.

"I am happy to meet you, Ben."

His eyes didn't leave her face, nor hers move from his. He reached up, helping her out of the carriage. She lifted the pink skirt, and still slipped on some mud. Ben bent down and scooped her into his arms and held her high as he walked over to a long plank leading up to the house. She was too shocked to even protest.

"There you go. Now it's your turn, Kate."

Kate laughed. "Ben, you silly thing, you."

Soon they were inside the small house, and introductions and greetings were made. Emily felt two pairs of eyes on her once her name was mentioned. She nodded slightly, holding her hand out to Mrs. Galloway.

"I'm so pleased to meet you."

"And I, you," the tall, raw-boned woman said. Her hand was warm and callused from many years of hard work. Emily liked her immediately.

The furnishings were meager, but there were enough chairs for everyone.

"This is temporary," Ben explained. "The new house should be finished end of next month." Even as he spoke, his eyes never left Emily's face. He could hardly believe she was here. And her cheeks all rosy and pink, matching the dress that flounced as she walked. What had happened to the gray and brown? Life had changed for her since she moved in with Kate. And he was glad for that.

A girl with waist length, thick hair stood up and smiled shyly. The hair. Emily couldn't help noticing how like her brother's her hair was. She wondered if his children would have hair like that, then stopped her thought mid-way. What on earth had led her to think about such things?

"Of course you'll have tea and some nice hot ginger-bread right out of the oven," Sarah Galloway said. "Baked it just a bit ago."

The room was warm. Cheery in spite of the lack of space.

Kate took over the conversation to Emily's relief. Emily was getting better, but still had a problem knowing what to say, especially when a certain pair of eyes stayed fastened on her. She didn't dare look in Ben's direction. She would really blush then.

"Do you like it in Oregon?" Kate was asking.

"Very much so. And my Ben was right about the rich earth. I have already planted onions, carrots, and corn. Radishes."

"Mom's a real gardener," Ben said. "She gets anything to grow."

Emily relaxed and reached out for the cup of steaming tea. Kurt who had been outside, came in and accepted his tea and gingerbread.

"I'd like to show you around," Ben said, his eyes still locked on Emily's. "I know where we can go to avoid most of the mud."

Emily nodded. "I would like that."

"Why did you come?" he asked once they were back out under the cloudless blue sky.

"I didn't know this was where I was coming."

"Oh. I knew there was a catch to it."

"But I would have wanted to come," Emily said. "I had to see you again to apologize for what I said that last time. It was entirely rude of me."

"You meant it though. About not caring."

"No, Ben, the words were not true."

He stopped walking and looked at her closely. Was she telling him something, or was it only his wishful thinking? How did one ever know?

She watched him out of the corner of her eye, wondering what he was thinking as a frown creased his brow.

"If the words spoken were not true, then what is the truth, Miss Emily Drake?"

"That I need not to only listen to my mind, but to my heart, also. The heart has its reasons, you know."

"And what does your heart tell you?"

"That I want to be your friend again."

His hopes and dreams seemed dashed against a cement wall. Friends. So all she wanted to be was friends. How could he convince her otherwise?

"I'm glad, Emily, for I will always be your friend."

Emily looked into his eyes, knowing she hoped to be more than friends. She wanted to tell Ben that he was in her morning thoughts, her afternoon thoughts, her evening thoughts. But to admit such a thing was too forward. It simply wasn't done.

Ben took her hand and held it gently. "I hear that friendship is a good base for lasting relationships. And my heart tells me to seek more. My God tells me I am ready for more."

Trembling, Emily's eyes met his and in the next second she was pulled into his arms as his head bent down and kissed the tip of her nose, first one cheek, then the other, and finally at last his mouth found hers. She felt pulled under and soon freed herself from his grasp.

"I'm sorry," Ben said. "Forgive me."

"Only if you forgive me first." A smile tugged at the corners of her mouth.

"Emily, is it possible that we might start over? Pretend the dance never happened?"

Emily felt her heart soaring. "I would like that, Ben. Yes, I would like that very much."

"I can come calling?"

"If you'd like. But I am going to California soon to see my family."

"You *are*?" He felt happy for her, knowing how important it was, but to lose her, even for a week, maybe longer, when he'd just found her troubled him.

As if reading his mind, she touched his arm. "I'm coming back, though. I promised Mr. Roberts."

"How about me?"

She smiled. "I can promise you, too."

"I'm building a house I want to show you." His eyes gazed into hers. "I think you'll like it."

"What sort of house?"

"It's large with a balcony on the second floor and big, wide rooms. One even has book shelves."

The meaning wasn't lost on Emily. "I would very much like to see your new house, Mr. Galloway."

He took her hand and together they walked out into the open, looking up at the blue, blue sky. Her spirit felt free as she lifted her face.

"'They that wait upon the Lord shall renew their strength,'" Emily started.

"'They shall mount up with wings as eagles,'" Ben said, finishing the phrase.

She turned to look at him. It was a sign. Her sign from God that yes, indeed, Ben *did* know Him.

Good-byes were said and the trio started on the homeward trek. Emily sat in the back, keeping the words, the thoughts, the sight of Ben tucked inside her heart. Her face glowed, her hands felt warm though it had grown cold and windy. Ben was coming tomorrow after work. She could ride in his carriage. She could talk to him on Kate's porch if she wanted. She might even wear the pink dress again. She felt free, yet she knew she would never be free from God's hand, God's rule on her life. And she didn't want to be.

Emily looked out from under the canopy at the heavens. "Thank You, dear God," she murmured. "I know You have guided me thus far and are certainly going to guide me even further." She finished the verse from Isaiah: "'They shall run and not be weary, and shall walk, and not faint.'"

She closed her eyes and saw Ben with his thick hair smiling at her and over him it was as if God held out His arms to both of them, encompassing them as one whole, as a committed pair willing and wanting to serve their Lord and Master.

A light rain began to fall. . .

A Letter To Our Readers

Dear Reader:

In order that we might better contribute to your reading enjoyment, we would appreciate your taking a few minutes to respond to the following questions. When completed, please return to the following:

Rebecca Germany, Editor
Heartsong Presents
P.O. Box 719
Uhrichsville, Ohio 44683

1. Did you enjoy reading *The Heart Has Its Reasons*?
   ❏ Very much. I would like to see more books
      by this author!
   ❏ Moderately
      I would have enjoyed it more if _____

   _____

2. Are you a member of *Heartsong Presents*?   Yes   No
   If no, where did you purchase this book? _____

   _____

3. What influenced your decision to purchase this
   book? (Check those that apply.)

   ❏ Cover   ❏ Back cover copy

   ❏ Title   ❏ Friends

   ❏ Publicity   ❏ Other _____

4. On a scale from 1 (poor) to 10 (superior), please rate the following elements.

___Heroine   ___Plot

___Hero   ___Inspirational theme

___Setting   ___Secondary characters

5. What settings would you like to see covered in *Heartsong Presents* books?

_____

_____

6. What are some inspirational themes you would like to see treated in future books?_____

_____

_____

7. Would you be interested in reading other *Heartsong Presents* titles?   ❑ Yes   ❑ No

8. Please check your age range:
❑ Under 18   ❑ 18-24   ❑ 25-34
❑ 35-45   ❑ 46-55   ❑ Over 55

9. How many hours per week do you read? _____

Name _____

Occupation _____

Address _____

City _____ State _____ Zip _____

···· Hearts ♥ ong ····

Any 12 *Heartsong Presents* titles for only $26.95 *

HISTORICAL ROMANCE IS CHEAPER BY THE DOZEN!

Buy any assortment of twelve *Heartsong Presents* titles and save 25% off of the already discounted price of $2.95 each!

plus $1.00 shipping and handling per order and sales tax where applicable.

HEARTSONG PRESENTS TITLES AVAILABLE NOW:

__HP 7 CANDLESHINE, *Colleen L. Reece*
__HP 8 DESERT ROSE, *Colleen L. Reece*
__HP 12 COTTONWOOD DREAMS, *Norene Morris*
__HP 15 WHISPERS ON THE WIND, *Maryn Langer*
__HP 16 SILENCE IN THE SAGE, *Colleen L. Reece*
__HP 23 GONE WEST, *Kathleen Karr*
__HP 24 WHISPERS IN THE WILDERNESS, *Colleen L. Reece*
__HP 27 BEYOND THE SEARCHING RIVER, *Jacquelyn Cook*
__HP 28 DAKOTA DAWN, *Lauraine Snelling*
__HP 31 DREAM SPINNER, *Sally Laity*
__HP 32 THE PROMISED LAND, *Kathleen Karr*
__HP 35 WHEN COMES THE DAWN, *Brenda Bancroft*
__HP 36 THE SURE PROMISE, *JoAnn A. Grote*
__HP 39 RAINBOW HARVEST, *Norene Morris*
__HP 40 PERFECT LOVE, *Janelle Jamison*
__HP 43 VEILED JOY, *Colleen L. Reece*
__HP 44 DAKOTA DREAM, *Lauraine Snelling*
__HP 47 TENDER JOURNEYS, *Janelle Jamison*
__HP 48 SHORES OF DELIVERANCE, *Kate Blackwell*
__HP 51 THE UNFOLDING HEART, *JoAnn A. Grote*
__HP 52 TAPESTRY OF TAMAR, *Colleen L. Reece*
__HP 55 TREASURE OF THE HEART, *JoAnn A. Grote*
__HP 56 A LIGHT IN THE WINDOW, *Janelle Jamison*
__HP 59 EYES OF THE HEART, *Maryn Langer*
__HP 60 MORE THAN CONQUERORS, *Kay Cornelius*
__HP 63 THE WILLING HEART, *Janelle Jamison*
__HP 64 CROWS'-NESTS AND MIRRORS, *Colleen L. Reece*
__HP 67 DAKOTA DUSK, *Lauraine Snelling*
__HP 68 RIVERS RUSHING TO THE SEA, *Jacquelyn Cook*
__HP 71 DESTINY'S ROAD, *Janelle Jamison*
__HP 72 SONG OF CAPTIVITY, *Linda Herring*
__HP 75 MUSIC IN THE MOUNTAINS, *Colleen L. Reece*
__HP 76 HEARTBREAK TRAIL, *VeraLee Wiggins*

(If ordering from this page, please remember to include it with the order form.)

·········· Presents ······

Great Inspirational Romance at a Great Price!

Heartsong Presents books are inspirational romances in contemporary and historical settings, designed to give you an enjoyable, spirit-lifting reading experience. You can choose from 124 wonderfully written titles from some of today's best authors like Colleen L. Reece, Brenda Bancroft, Janelle Jamison, and many others.

When ordering quantities less than twelve, above titles are $2.95 each.

HeartsꞋng Presents
Love Stories Are Rated G!

That's for godly, gratifying, and of course, great! If you love a thrilling love story, but don't appreciate the sordidness of popular paperback romances, **Heartsong Presents** is for you. In fact, **Heartsong Presents** is the *only inspirational romance book club*, the only one featuring love stories where Christian faith is the primary ingredient in a marriage relationship.

Sign up today to receive your first set of four, never before published Christian romances. Send no money now; you will receive a bill with the first shipment. You may cancel at any time without obligation, and if you aren't completely satisfied with any selection, you may return the books for an immediate refund!

Imagine. . .four new romances every month—two historical, two contemporary—with men and women like you who long to meet the one God has chosen as the love of their lives. . .all for the low price of $9.97 postpaid.

To join, simply complete the coupon below and mail to the address provided. **Heartsong Presents** romances are rated G for another reason: They'll arrive *Godspeed!*